DONUT LEAVE ME

TERESA CRUMPTON

Teresa Crumpton
xx ox

❀ Created with Vellum

INTRODUCTION

Dear Reader,

June 1st is National Donut Day. To celebrate this amazing dessert, a baker's dozen of authors have come together to create thirteen new stories that are sugar-free and donut contain carbs!
Each story is a complete standalone. They vary in theme and heat levels.
We hope you enjoy the donut day collaboration and that we bring you a little something to help satisfy your sweet tooth.
Please consider reviewing to help your authors.
Enjoy!

With love and sprinkles,
Donut Day Authors

DEDICATION

To all my nieces: This is for you, with love.

CHAPTER 1

Forest

IT'S TOO DAMN EARLY for someone to be knocking on my door. I reach for my my phone to see what time it is. If it's before 10 AM I'm not going to answer. The screen reads 9:40 AM.

"Go the fuck away, and let me sleep," I growl, knowing damn well the person pounding on my door can't hear me.

"Are you going to get that?" the woman next to me mumbles, and for the life of me, I can't remember her name.

She's the first woman I've brought back to my place in weeks. I toss the covers off and slip out of bed, grabbing my sweats off the floor and stepping into them as I stumble my way to the front door. There are shuffling sounds coming from my room, and I guess my one night stand is getting dressed. Thank fuck I won't have to kick her out when I go back to bed.

I glance through the peephole and freeze. The chick knocking on my door looks vaguely familiar, but if this is who I'm thinking she might be, I haven't seen her in years. Somewhere around eight years I'd guess. Hell, I've even moved since then. A few times. I flip the locks and unchain the door before opening it.

It's fucking bright out, so I have to squint at the woman. "Can I help you?"

"Forest?" she asks, wrapping her arms over her chest. "Forest Jenson?"

I swear this can't be who she reminds me of. Hallie had curves that wouldn't quit and was built. This woman is practically skin and bones.

"I'm Forest Jenson. Is there something I can do for you?" I'm hoping she'll actually tell me why she's at my door this time, and I can answer her question and get back in my bed soon. It's too early for this shit.

"Sorry, yes. May I come in? This conversation would be better if you're sitting down," she continues, but I'm leery of letting her in my apartment. "Also... Uh... can I ask you to put on a shirt? This discussion is going to be difficult enough without staring at your chest and tattoos."

I glance down at myself and shrug. The woman has balls, I'll give her that. The fact that I'm not sure if I know her is only one reason I hesitate. The other reason has to do with the crazy-ass bitch my friend and coworker, Wes, is dating. I don't want to invite that brand of crazy into my home. But looking at this woman and her frailty makes me think better of leaving her standing on the stoop. I open the door wider and step back, giving her a silent invitation and space to enter.

The chick from my bed walks out of my room. She's completely rumpled. *Walk of shame doesn't look good on you.*

"Umm. I'm going to go," she mumbles, grabbing her purse and coverup on the way out.

"Sure." I continue to hold the door open for her.

"I'm so sorry. I didn't realize you had company," my new guest apologizes. "I should go. Maybe this was a bad idea." She bites her bottom lip and turns to head toward the door I'm still holding open.

I hold up my hand in the universal "stop" signal at her. There is no fucking way I'm letting her leave now. I'm all too curious to hear what she has to say at this point.

My date from last night steps outside and tells me over her shoulder, "I left my number next to your phone. Call me."

"Sure." She turns and saunters off, and I close the door behind her then face the newcomer. "Now what can I do for you?"

"Your... uh shirt... please?" She walks toward the couch.

"Seriously? You come to *my* place, get me out of my warm bed too damn early, and you want *me* to put on a shirt?"

"Yes. Please?"

"Fine," I grumble at her. "Do you know how to make coffee? I think I'm going to need it. You start the coffee, I'll get my shirt on." I raise my eyebrow at her.

She nods, places her purse on my coffee table, and points in the direction she assumes my kitchen is with raised eyebrows as if asking for my confirmation.

Wonder if she knows how to make French press coffee? Screw it. I'm not even going to ask.

"Yeah, kitchen's that way," I nod in the direction she's pointing, "and the coffee should be on the counter. I have a Keurig, so make yourself a cup too if you'd like. By the way, you wanna tell me your name?"

She stops dead in her tracks and very slowly faces me. "You don't remember my name?"

"Lady, I barely remember my own some days and, while you look oddly familiar, the person you remind me of I haven't seen in about eight years." I cross my arms over my chest, still waiting for her answer.

"You're right. Good point. Fuck. This really is going to be harder than I thought." She blows out a long breath. "Forget the shirt, and you're gonna want something stronger than coffee. Can I sit?" She motions to my couch.

I nod and move to lean against the doorframe, my arms remaining crossed. Something feels off with this chick, and I'm beginning to think it was a bad idea to let her in.

She lets out another breath as she takes a seat. "I had this awesome speech prepared, but that was when I thought you'd recognize me. I realize I look nothing like what I used to. Well, 'nothing' isn't really the right term, but…. Anyway, my name is Hallie Hartley." Hearing her name nearly stops my heart. This frail woman can't be Hallie. She keeps talking, and I'm pretty damn sure I've missed something she's said. "I know we lost contact after that one night, but I'm still best friends with your sister, Piper. In fact, she's the reason I'm here."

"Hallie Hartley." I stare at her, my arms falling to my sides as I push off the doorframe. Now that I know it's her, I can see more of her features that I remember. But still… she's so frail. "It's been years. Why did Piper send you to me now?" *What the hell are you doing, Piper?*

"Yeah, it's been seven years and about nine months, to be exact. The night of Nessa's engagement, Piper drug me out to celebrate with everyone." She rubs the back of her neck, the gesture pulling my attention to her hair. It's a *lot* different than it used to be.

It had been long and lush; now it's in a cute pixie cut and not really something I'd picture a cheerleader having. *Is she still a cheerleader? Didn't Piper say Hallie had joined her squad?*

"Seven or eight years sounds about right. Not to be rude, but I'm not really understanding why Piper, or you, would want to have this walk down memory lane after all this time. If I remember right, two weeks after our night together you were trying out to be a professional cheerleader with my sister."

"I did. And I made the team, in fact. At least for part of a season. But a few months later, I had to quit." She stares down at her hands as she fidgets with them, and there's this long, awkward pause before she speaks again.

"I... uh... couldn't cheer and be pregnant at the same time," she confesses so quietly that I'm not really sure I hear her right.

"Pregnant?" I choke out, my voice shaky even to my own ears. I cross my arms again as if to protect myself. *Shit! Dammit! FUCK! This can NOT be happening!* "Hallie...." My voice cracks so I clear my throat and try again. "What the hell are you here to tell me? Are you telling me that... uh that one night we spent together...." My voice is stronger now. "Holy hell! You got pregnant that night?!" I roar. "And why the fuck are you just *now* telling me?" She flinches, and I know my tone sounds harsher than I want it to, but I can't help that. I'm quickly moving from stunned to pissed.

"Yes." She speaks the word softly and meekly, which is nothing like I remember Hallie being. "Even with all of our precautions, somehow I got pregnant that night. I didn't say anything to you because by the time I realized it, I was dating someone else. Plus, I wasn't living anywhere near you. You had a good job, and so did I, and I didn't want to mess that up for either of us," Hallie admits, glancing at me but unwilling to keep eye contact.

There's no fucking way I have a child!

"So you figured what? I wouldn't want to know I had a child? That I wouldn't support you both? That I wouldn't try to make us a family? That I'd deprive you, and *my* child, of a

6

stable home?" I snarl, my temper flaring again as I begin to pace.

"It wasn't like that Forest, I swear! I knew you'd do anything for your family, but I also knew you loved working with your friends. Piper talked about everything you were doing... daily. And, no she didn't know I was pregnant with *your* child. So please don't be pissed at her," Hallie pleads with tortured eyes.

Knowing that little bit helps calm me slightly, but Piper has to know something now for her to send Hallie to me at this point.

"Look, I wanted to raise Isabella, I call her Ella, myself, and yes, it's been hard. But I thought it would be best for everyone. Did I make a bad decision? Possibly. But your life was here, and mine was not. I'm a cheerleader, and a sports trainer. My life was with the team I was working for, and your life was here... cooking. I'm sorry."

"So what? *Now* you need my help?" I glower at her as I pace.

"Ella and I both need your help," she admits sadly, and I stop dead in my tracks.

Why would they both need my help? I take a moment to look more closely at Hallie and realize I can see her bones, she's so thin. Even for a cheerleader, she's too thin. And for the first time, I really notice what's she's wearing. It's August here in Austin, and she's in long pants and a form-fitting, long-sleeved shirt.

"Why Hallie? Why do y'all need my help *now*?"

"Because..." she hesitates. "...I'm dying, Forest. And I'd rather our daughter be with *you* than in a foster home, or even with my family, for that matter," Hallie finishes, finally making eye contact with me and holding it.

"Fuck!" My throat goes dry, and I swallow hard.

"You can say that again." She scratches her hair and all of it shifts slightly. I must stare at her head for longer than I think because Hallie explains, "It's a wig. One of many. I lost all my hair during chemo."

Cancer?! Mother. Fucker!

"I'm sorry." I'm finally able to force the words out. "How long have you been sick?" I'm at a total loss as to how to deal with all of this. I'm still pissed, because how many sucker-punches to the gut can I take in one conversation? But... she's dying, so I shouldn't be so harsh.

"They found the ovarian cancer while I was pregnant with Ella. During the pregnancy they couldn't do much to treat it, mainly because I wasn't willing to give up Ella. The doctors told me she might be the only biological child I could have, depending on the treatment. And, against their better judgement, I decided to keep her." Tears fill Hallie's eyes as I move closer to her and the couch.

"You- you kept our baby, despite what the doctors told you?" I'm floored and in awe of her bravery. My temper quickly deflates.

"Yeah. Piper was there for that part, but I still didn't tell her the baby was her niece or nephew," she chuckles softly.

I slowly ease myself down next to her on the couch. "I'm

sorry you went through all that without help besides my sister. Hallie, I'm really trying to understand why you waited this long to tell me about our child. Especially knowing you were sick. Am I on her birth certificate?"

"No," she admits, quickly adding, "But only because I didn't want Piper to find out you are Ella's father. I didn't think she'd respect my wishes and not tell you. Or Nessa for that matter. Right after Ella was born, the doctors told me I wouldn't have long. But... then they were hopeful that I would have more years because I'd started treatments and, for a while, they worked. Obviously I'm not that lucky, though. The cancer returned, and the treatments aren't working anymore." Her voice is shaky, and I watch as tears begin to fall. "When they told me the cancer was back, I knew I'd made the right decision not to tell you, only so that I could have that short amount of time with Ella all to myself. Yes, it was extremely selfish, but I knew you'd have so many more years with her." She's sobbing now, and tears keep rolling down her face as she's trying to wipe them away.

"Dammit Hallie," I whisper. I want to say more, but in some respects I can understand why she did what she did. Hell, I don't even know if I'd have done anything differently if I was her. *Still....*

"I know." She deflates a little more, and I can see the toll this conversation is taking on her. "In the short time I have left, I want to help get you and Ella settled."

I run my hand through my hair. "Fuck. Hallie, how do

you expect me to get settled with Ella when I've never even met her? Not to mention, my life is here in Austin and, if I remember right, you live down in Houston."

"Piper wasn't wrong when she told me to do this sooner," she mumbles.

I interrupt her before she can say more. "How long has my sister known I have a child? And I want the truth," I bite out.

"Before I answer that, know that Piper wanted me to tell you the truth as soon as she found out, but I'm the one that wouldn't let her share anything with you. That's also the reason she doesn't call much. After Ella was born, and I started treatment, Piper and I moved in together. It made sense to me, because Ella would be with family even if Piper didn't know Ella was her niece. As Ella got older, more of your family's features started showing on her, and Piper put two and two together. She was pissed, but at the same time, we were just finding out that the cancer was more aggressive than the doctors originally thought. That was about five years ago."

"Piper's known for five fucking years?" I yell, popping off the couch to pace some more.

"Yes, and she and I have a monthly fight over that fact. Last year she talked me into looking at jobs here in Austin. About three months ago, I was offered a position at the University. I took it as a sign. However, it turns out it wasn't the sign I was hoping for. Two weeks ago at my last check up, the doctors said the treatments weren't working anymore, and the cancer is spreading."

I stop pacing and spin to face her, my fight leaving me just that quickly once again. "Hallie, I'm so fucking sorry."

She shrugs as if resigned to the fact she is dying. "It is what it is. Ella and I have been in the city for a little over three weeks so we could get settled in before I start my first day on the job. I'm in talks with the University to see if Piper can take over my position soon. During the off-seasons, she went back to school to finish her education to be a sports trainer. After I got my job, she thought it might be a good idea to see if she could find a job here as well, to help with the transition. We just didn't realize this would all happen so quickly."

My breath catches, and I try to clear my throat, but it won't clear. "Three weeks, and I'm just now seeing you?" I run my hand through my hair. "You want Ella to stay with Piper?" *I am so confused.*

"No, sorry. This is all coming out so jumbled," she huffs out. Taking a deep breath, she continues. "What I mean is, I think Ella needs to be with you, not Piper. I'm just saying you'll have someone that Ella knows close by." Hallie glances around my apartment. "I might suggest you move in to my place, though, and take over the lease. That is, if you're up for it. It will keep things a little more stable for Ella."

"I'll think about it. I realize this place isn't big enough for a child and myself." Scrubbing my face with my hands, I'm not sure what the *fuck* to do. I'm not just pissed beyond belief with both Hallie *and* Piper, but I'm also overwhelmed learning I have a daughter. And I'm *for sure* still in shock. My hands are shaking as I remove them from my face.

I take a deep breath. "I'd like to meet Ella, and start whatever procedures I need to so we can start making her legally mine. No matter how pissed I am at you and Piper, I'm not going to take that out on your... *our*... little girl. I have to work tonight and, I know this makes me sound like a complete asshole, but I need some time to process the fact that I have a daughter, along with everything else you've thrown at me. Not to mention I need a stiff drink." *Or four.* I look down at my watch before it registers that I'm not wearing it. "I'm betting it's still too early for that, though."

She nods. "You're right. It is a little early. How about you give me your number, and I can text you a couple pictures of Ella then set up a time where we can all meet? I've been gathering all the legal documents to give you custody. The last thing that's needed is a DNA test. Piper did one behind my back years ago, and it proved you're her father. However, it would be better if you submitted one too, so there are no issues later."

"That sounds good." I rattle off my number for her, but it still feels as if I'm disconnected from my brain.

My phone buzzes in the other room.

"That's probably me. I sent you a picture." Hallie reaches for her purse. "I should get going."

She stands and heads for the door, stopping when she's next to me, and places her hand on my arm. "Forest, thanks for hearing me out. And for not kicking me out before I could tell you everything." She looks exhausted, and now that I'm this close to her, I can see the dark circles under her eyes that I hadn't paid attention to when she first walked in.

"You were expecting the worst weren't you?" I smirk slightly.

"Piper told me to stay optimistic, but considering every-thing…. It's a lot. And normally you only ever hear the horror stories about situations like this. I didn't want that for Ella. Or for you. So, thank you." She rises up on her tiptoes and kisses my cheek. "Call me when you're ready. I'll show myself out."

Before I can respond, the door is closing softly behind her.

"Fuck me!" I shout as I unconsciously move into the kitchen for my coffee.

I have a kid. A fucking seven-year-old daughter. I'm going to fucking kill Piper. Damn… Nessa might beat me to it. Shit! I'm going to be a single parent. What the fuck am I going to do? I don't have the slightest idea how to be a parent!

The ringing of my cell phone brings me out of my thoughts. I need coffee, and I need it *now*. Whoever is calling can wait until I've had a cup. *Or five.*

CHAPTER 2

Hallie

That went better than I expected. Piper was right... I am
a fucking selfish bitch.

I left Forest standing dumbfounded in his
living room. I'm not even sure if it registered with him that I
was leaving. By the end of the conversation, I'm not sure he
was even listening to me. Piper warned me that might
happen. She'd said there was a possibility he could just shut
down. I can't really blame him for it. I mean, it's not like he
finds out every day he has a seven-year-old daughter he
knew nothing about.

Speaking of Piper, I need to call her and let her know I've
spoken to Forest. And that he wasn't too happy with his baby
sister. As I walk down the stairs toward my truck, I pull out

my cell and dial her.

The phone rings four times before she answers. "How'd he take it?"

"Well, hello to you too. Your brother asked a few questions. He's a little pissed at you, I think, and when I left, he wasn't talking at all," I reply, pulling my keys out of my pocket and pushing the unlock button.

There is silence, so I pull the phone from my ear to check if we've gotten disconnected- we haven't. "Piper?"

"Sorry, I uh… fuck," Piper mutters. "Do you still want me to come up this weekend? If my brother is pissed at me, I'm not sure my presence will help, but it might draw Nessa's attention away from the situation."

"Honestly, I think Ella would be happier if you were here. She hasn't said anything, but I think she misses you and the team."

"I'm heading to practice now. I'll talk to everyone and let them know I'm heading up today. I'd rather get the wrath of my siblings out of the way." She groans.

"Are you sure? I don't want to screw up the training schedule." I open my door and slide into the seat, closing the door as I settle in.

"I'm sure. I want Ella to feel safe. Besides, I'm the one that's been telling her about Forest. Do you want me to bring anything up? Donuts? Or have you guys found a place for your weekly donut fix yet?" Piper responds.

"You have a point. We haven't had much of a chance to explore things. Between getting settled in the house, my new job, getting the legal papers started, and all the doctors' appointments, we've been homebodies. Donuts would probably put a smile on Ella's face, but don't go overboard. Just grab two or something, and we'll find a local place on Saturday." My stomach twists at the thought that I won't have our weekly donut dates much longer.

Fuck! This has to be my punishment for not telling Forest about Ella from the beginning.

"I'll be there in about six hours. Love ya girl. I gotta go, just got to practice," Piper announces and we disconnect.

I toss my phone in a cup holder and start the engine. As I begin to back out of the parking spot an alarm sounds from my phone.

Damnit, I didn't bring my meds.

I head back toward the house in the hopes that I get there before the nausea overtakes me. Halfway down the street I have to pull over, and I barely make it out of the vehicle before I'm throwing up.

Shit! Today is going to be bad. I haven't gotten sick that quickly in a while. Maybe today wasn't the day to go see Forest.

Slowly, I get back in my car and search for something to wipe off my face. Of course it's in the very last spot I look. After I clean my face, I grab my water from the cup holder and take a swig. Once I'm resituated, I put the car in gear and drive home as fast as I legally can.

I arrive home and sprint to my bathroom as the need to hurl consumes me. I make it to the toilet just in time. When everything has been expelled from my stomach, I clean myself up again and search for my anti-nausea pills.

In the kitchen, I find the meds on the counter. Opening the bottle, I shake one pill into my hand before resealing the container. Walking over to the fridge, I grab a water bottle and pop the pill in my mouth, taking a swig of water with it. Glancing at the time on the microwave, my tardiness dawns.

Shit! I need to get to work.

The drive over to the University, while slower than my mad dash home, is blissfully uneventful.

Ella

I SWEAR this is the longest day of my *life*. Every time I look at the clock above the whiteboard it says almost the exact same time. I don't want to be at school today. At *all*. I wanted to go with Mom. I overheard her talking to Aunt Piper when she thought I was in bed. Mom said she was going to see Aunt Piper's brother, my daddy, and tell him about me. Before we moved here, Aunt Piper would tell me all about her brother.

'Forest is a pretty cool dude for a brother. The best part is, he makes theses amazing desserts,' she'd say, especially when she'd bake me chocolate chip cookies from a package.

She'd tell me, *"Your daddy would never make these. He'd make them from scratch. In fact, never tell him I made these for you. He might not let me in the kitchen again."* Then she'd wink. Aunt Piper doesn't like to cook all that much.

It's been a month since I've seen Aunt Piper, or any of my friends. I had been looking forward to starting second grade with my friends from first grade. But now I'm here, and I *haaate* it. I don't know anyone, and everyone keeps asking me about my daddy. *It sucks.* The only thing I know to tell them is that he's a pastry chef. Aunt Piper made sure I knew that. She also showed me a picture of him from when they were kids. I liked the picture. I got to see my other aunt, too. She's Daddy's twin, though they don't look like twins.

Come on bell, ring already!!! I'm boooooored!

"Class, let's line up for music," my teacher tells us, and my classmates run to the door.

I'm not in a hurry to get to music. I love to sing and play the piano, but lately it just makes me sad. Mom keeps saying she wants me to have a *normal* life. She always makes this gesture with her fingers when she says the normal part. Aunt Piper always tells her its effing stupid, that I don't have a normal life and never will. I know she really wants to say a bad word, but she tries really hard not to when I might hear. It makes me laugh because then she'll say, *"Your daddy would kick my ass."*

I really want to meet him soooonnnn! He sounds like a great Daddy. But I can't imagine him kicking Aunt Piper's ass. I've seen her work out with the team, and I've even practiced with her. She tells me all the time I'd make an awesome cheerleader. At Mom's old work, a few people called me a *natural...* whatever that means.

As my mind wanders, I'm not paying attention to the boy

in front of me, and I accidentally run into him when he stops.

"Hey." He pushes me back. I know better than to react. Growing up around all the football players taught me not to. They also taught me how to stick up for myself, even at my age.

One day the guys got all of us kids out on the field, and we practiced with them. Well, not really practiced. They did show us how to play football and, of course, they made sure the girls could throw a punch. That was *soooo* much fun.

The boy pushes me again. All morning he's been in my face and, if I wouldn't get in trouble, I'd punch him like the players taught me.

"Alexander, face the front," the teacher calls out, and the line moves down the hall.

As we get to the music room, Ms. Scott stops me after everyone else goes into the room. "Ella, are you okay today? You seem a little distracted. I know it's only your second day, and you're just getting to know everyone." I think Ms. Scott is going to say more but she doesn't. She waits a second then steps aside and lets me go to class.

"Yes, ma'am. I'm fine," I answer her as I walk into the music room.

"Ohhhh Ella got in trouble," the annoying boy calls out.

"Alexander, that is not polite, and I will not tolerate anymore of that behavior in my classroom," Ms. Cook, our music teacher, says. "Do you understand?"

"Yes, Ms. Cook," Alexander answers, taking a seat next to his friends.

"Ella, I have you sitting next to Payton." She points to an open spot, and I walk over to it and take a seat.

Ms. Cook explains the lesson before having us stand and find an instrument. We're all supposed to find a different instrument, but everyone wants to play on the drums. I roll my eyes. Drums are boring, and I'd rather play the piano at the back of the room. While Ms. Cook is distracted, I drift over to it and sit on the bench. Music starts to play in the room, and while the rhythm isn't great, my fingers itch to play. I hear her give more instructions to the class, and I all I want is to drown out all the noise. As the song changes, I flex my fingers and place them gently on the ivory keys. My eyes close as I listen to the song, *A Thousand Years,* and begin to play along with it. I've played it a few times, so it's not hard to keep up. In fact, I sing softly along with it.

I'm so focused on the notes that I don't notice when the room goes silent. And it does go completely quiet. But I keep playing after the song ends, morphing the melody into something completely different.

"Ella. Ella!" Ms. Cook calls. My eyes open and, by the expressions on everyone's faces, I think I'm in trouble.

"Yes, ma'am," I say, standing so I can move away from the piano.

"Please... sit back down." She starts to move over to the piano. "Could you not hear me calling your name?" she wonders.

I sit on the edge of the bench so I can see her. "Sorry, no ma'am. When I get lost in the music, I zone out."

"Class, please take a seat," Ms. Cook directs. "Ella, can you play anything you hear on the piano?" Her expression is one I've seen on Mom and Aunt Piper when they're trying to figure out what all I can do when I'm practicing cheerleading with them.

"No ma'am, but I know this song. I've played it a few times, but I play it better on my keyboard, since I don't have to reach the pedals," I reply, gently kicking my feet back and forth under my seat, the tip of my shoes barely scraping the tile floor.

"That makes sense. Can you read sheet music?" she wants to know, stepping around a few of my classmates to get closer to me.

"Yes, ma'am. I've taken lessons," I inform her.

She comes to stand next to the bench, and I scoot over to give her space to sit next to me. She takes sheet music off the top of the piano and lays it in front of us. I don't recognize the title, but I can't say that's unusual for me. I know songs, but I don't always know their titles.

"Will you play this with me?" Ms. Cook asks.

I nod and, reading the notes, I begin to play. It's not long before I realize I do know the song, and I glance up at the title. *Way Down We Go*. It's one of Mom and Aunt Piper's favorites. I've played it a few times. We normally sing along with it. Ms. Cook stops playing on the keys and just pushes the pedals for me.

I finish the song, and she looks down at me. "We have time for one more song. Are you willing to try it too?"

I nod again.

She flips through a few sheets until she comes to another one she wants. For this one, I recognize the name of the band, The Fray. This time, however, Ms. Cook rests her hands in her lap, only working the pedals for me as I play. When I finish, there are more adults standing by the door.

"Excuse me, Ms. Cook? I don't mean to interrupt, but I really need to get the class back to our room," Ms. Scott tells her.

"Yes, of course. I thought we had a little longer, but I lost track of time. Class, line up please. Ella, thank you for playing." She rises from the bench, and I scoot out, heading for the back of the line again.

From somewhere up the line I hear a boy's voice say, "She's a show-off."

"That was cool," Payton, the girl in front of me, whispers.

"Thank you," I whisper back and chew on my lip.

Why can't I be back with my friends at my old school? They were fun and a lot cooler than these kids. Well, except maybe Payton.

We walk back to class. Faint whispers from my fellow classmates, and hushed instructions as we pass other classrooms, are my only distractions. Otherwise, I keep wondering what Mom is saying to my dad. *I wonder if I can meet him today? If he'll teach me to cook? What he might make me the first time we meet?*

My questions are endless, really, but there are two questions I really want to ask, but I'm scared to learn the answers. *Why didn't he come find us? And will he love and want me?*

When we get into class I head straight for my desk, but Ms. Scott's words stop me in my tracks.

"Class, if you brought your lunch, please grab it and line back up. We have five minutes to get to the cafeteria, and we'll stop at the bathroom on the way."

Maybe lunch will get me in a better mood.

CHAPTER 3

Forest

By the time I make it into Belladonna, I'm running an hour late. I'm distracted and really want a drink--or four. As I burst through the front doors, I'm met by Adam, my brother-in-law.

"Hey man, you okay? Nessa said some shit went down this morning?" He's handing me a mug of piping hot coffee. "I spiked it."

"Thanks, I need this." I take a sip as I head to the kitchen. "Is everyone here?"

"Just the normal crew, minus your sister. She had an appointment. Calla, Trey, Wes, and a few of the kitchen staff are all here, though. Why do you ask?" Adam questions as he starts toward the bar.

"You'll want to hear what I need to tell everyone," I tell him as I pass the bar.

Adam nods. "I'll just grab a bottle in case we need it."

"Good idea." I push through the kitchen door.

The kitchen is already in full swing as dinner is being prepared for the staff. It's one of the personal touches Calla does to make Belladonna feel more like a family than just a job. When she first started the practice, I didn't think it would last. But she's proven me wrong, even after the shit her ex pulled. Eight months ago, I really worried about the family aspect going away after Calla's life got thrown into disarray.

Torrance, the asshole ex, had a hand in some of the decisions Calla made for the restaurant, considering they were engaged at the time. Now the fucker is with some tart, and has been since before they'd broken up. Though none of us knew that until the night they broke up. Everything has suffered since that night, but Calla's cooking has suffered the most.

As her family, we are the ones closest to her. Because we love her, we've picked up the slack without her having to ask, allowing Calla to heal in her own way, and in her own time. *I just hope she gets her mojo back, and soon, because she was... IS... an awesome chef.*

Finishing my coffee, I head directly to my work space to start prepping for the desserts I'll fix tonight.

"Hey Forest? Everything okay?" Calla calls out as she walks over to Trey's station.

"Haha, yeah... let's just say it's been a day," I respond, pulling out my bowls.

"You going to tell us about it over dinner?" she wants to know.

"Yep." I step away from my counter to grab the ingredients I'll need for the New York-style cheesecake, pudding for the fruit tart, and chocolate cake.

"Alright y'all, dinner is ready. Let's go eat!" Trey calls out.

Fuck! I'm already in the fucking weeds.

"I'll be there in twenty. Let me start the batter," I call back.

"Let's eat dinner while it's hot. I'll help with the batter later," Wes offers as he steps up next to my station.

"Thanks, Wes." I follow everyone out into the dining room to a grouping of tables in the center of the room.

Per usual, a few tables have been pushed together for our family-style meal. We all take a seat, and Adam sits next to me, placing a highball glass and a bottle in front of me. I glance around, noticing a few raised eyebrows. Drinking before shift is highly abnormal for me. It's abnormal for everyone here. Sure we let loose, have fun, and give each other shit, but drinks don't happen until after shift. However, even when we go out, I usually only have one drink.

Pour the whiskey and blurt it out.

I listen to my inner self, pouring a double. Instead of blurting out to my friends... my family... I have a seven-year-old daughter, I pick up the glass and toss back the whiskey. Then I speak.

"I have a daughter," I confess as I place the empty glass on the table.

Drinks and a bit of food spew across the table. *Guess I should've seen that coming.*

"You what? I didn't know you were even dating anyone seriously. Ness is going to have a field day," Adam spits out as he fills his glass with whiskey as well.

Yeah, she will since they'd been trying to get pregnant for a year with no luck. My twin is amazingly strong. I don't know if I'd keep trying.

"Yeah, I just found out this morning. And to add fuel to that fire, she's seven years old, and her name is Isabella. Her mom calls her Ella for short." More drinks spew across the table, and this time I have to dry myself off with a towel.

"You have a what?" Calla's ire is in full swing. "I couldn't have heard you right... a seven-year-old? Where the fuck did she come from?"

"Well, it seems the one-night stand I had with Piper's friend, Hallie, all those years ago ended up with her getting pregnant. She's been sick with cancer since then, so she wanted to spend as much time as she could with Ella before she dies. The doctors give her six months."

"You're getting a DNA test before you agree to this. And this is just shitty of her, by the way," Calla states. The look on her face tells me that if I don't agree to the test, she'll drag my ass to a doctor's office.

"Hold up! Piper's friend? You mean the one that lives with her and works with her? That friend?" Adam chimes in.

I nod.

"Oh hell. Ness's going to kill Piper. I really don't want to have conjugal visits with your sister in jail. That just doesn't work for me," Adam states, only half joking.

"Dude, I really don't need you even remotely telling me about having sex with my twin," I respond, shaking my head, trying to rid myself of the images now in my brain. "Now that I need to scrub that picture from my mind, yes Calla, I plan on getting a DNA test. In fact, Hallie even suggested it. And no, Piper never told me, either."

"Well damn. How are you doing with the news?" Trey makes a grab for the whiskey bottle. "I think I need one of these, too."

"Pour all of us one. We definitely need it," Calla encourages, holding out a glass for the amber liquid.

Trey does Calla's bidding. When we all have our drinks, my family toasts me as they would if I was dating someone and found out she was pregnant.

"Honestly, I'm not sure how I feel. I'm pissed for missing out on seven years of her life. And for not being given an opportunity to have a family. I'm scared shitless that Ella'll think I didn't want her, or that she won't like me. On the flip side, I want to know what she looks like, what she does for fun, what music she listens to, and what movies she watches. And most importantly, what desserts she loves, and will she want to learn to cook?"

The table falls silent after I respond to Trey's question. I sip my drink and take a few bites of the meal my friends prepared. All the fears I've just spoken out loud run through my mind. *I wonder if all fathers have these fears when they find out they're going to be a dad?*

I'm still pondering my last thought as a buzzing intrudes on my musings. We all glance at our phones. Mine's flashing a number I don't recognize.

"It's me." I hit accept. "Hello?"

"Mr. Jenson?" an unfamiliar voice questions.

"Yeah, that's me." It comes out as more of a question than a statement.

"Mr. Jenson, I'm Officer Brown. There was an accident, and your name is the emergency contact for a Hallie Hartley," the man tells me.

I push back from the table and hold up a finger as I walk away.

"What kind of accident, officer? Was there a little girl with her?" I quiz him.

"It was a motor vehicle accident. Ms. Hartley was hit in the driver's side door. She's being taken to St. David's North Hospital. She was alone in the vehicle."

"Shit! I need to find Ella. Thank you for calling. I'll be at the hospital as soon as I can," I respond before disconnecting the call.

I jog back to the table. "Hallie was in an accident, and I don't have a fucking clue what school my daughter attends."

"Call Piper. I bet she knows what school Ella goes to," Adam says pulling his phone out as I run a hand through my hair.

My hands shake as I take the phone from Adam. It rings three times before Piper picks up.

"Adam, is Nessa okay?" my baby sister begins without even saying hello.

"Piper," I start, but before I can say more, she interrupts me.

"Forest, why are you calling from Adam's phone? What happened?" Her voice shakes as she speaks.

"Nessa and Adam are fine. Hallie was in an accident. She's been taken to St. David's. Ella wasn't in the car with Hallie, so I need to find her."

"Oh fuck! No, no, no!" Piper mutters, not answering my question. I want to scream my frustration out at my sister. My little girl is at school, and I have to meet her for the first time and tell her that her mom is hurt all at once.

"Piper, damnit! My daughter is at school, and I don't know which one!" I growl into the phone.

"Shit... Ella! I'll get her. Meet me at the hospital. Which one did you say they are taking Hallie to?"

"How the fuck will you get Ella?" I demand, pacing.

"I'm already in town. Hallie wanted me here when you met Ella. I'm on the highway about to take the next exit to Hallie's house. Now which hospital?"

I let out a long breath, grateful Piper is here and able to help me meet my daughter for the very first time. Thankfully, Hallie had already thought to call her in.

"She's at St. David's North. I'm at Belladonna, and it's going to take me a hot minute to get there, even on my bike."

"Get out of the damn way fucker!" Piper yells at another driver, I assume. "Forest, just get to the hospital. This could be bad for Hallie."

That stops me dead in my tracks. "What do you mean?"

"Let's just see how she is when we get to the hospital. I gotta go. I'm pulling into the school parking lot now." She disconnects.

With my keys in hand, I realize my friends have gathered around me, and Calla also has her things with her.

"Come on, let's go. I'm driving," Calla directs, nodding toward the door.

Adam has his hand out for his phone, and I drop it in his palm. "Calla, I'm fine."

"No, you're really not, so I'm driving. Your daughter needs her father now more than ever. Besides, we all know my cooking has been shit lately. Trey and Wes can handle the kitchen just fine without me, and Adam and Nessa, when she gets in, will handle the front of the house. Now get in my fucking Jeep," she growls at me.

I can't argue with her, and the fact that she realizes her cooking has been shit is just one of the reasons she's one of my favorite people. It takes a strong person to see their issues, and an even stronger one to admit something is flawed. Calla is doing both, as I know she's been trying to work out her issues and get her cooking mojo back.

"Fine, you win. I'll let you drive." I head for the front door.

"Calla, take my car. It's faster than yours." I turn back around to see Trey giving his keys to Calla.

"Good point. I don't need him bitching at me to go faster," she mutters. Everyone chuckles as she jogs in my direction.

"Thanks y'all." I reach the door and push it open for Calla to exit first. We step into the heat of the late afternoon and scramble to Trey's sports car.

CHAPTER 4

Forest

CALLA PULLS into the parking lot of St. David's North Hospital within fifteen minutes. The fact that she didn't get a ticket while driving here is shocking. Granted, she did get pulled over, but when she explained to the officer why she'd been speeding, he immediately escorted us here.

"Thank you, officer," I throw over my shoulder as I dart through the Emergency Room doors.

I'm in line at the counter before Calla and the officer make it inside. *Is he going to check our story?* The officer walks past me and over to a door to my right as Calla comes to stand next to me.

"I'm going to find us seats while we wait," she announces and strolls off.

The line to speak to the intake nurse is slow as fuck, and the wait is killing me. Pulling out my phone, I check to see if I have any messages from Piper. I have none, and the fact that I'm not getting service in here could be the cause of it. *Motherfucker.* I slide my phone back in to my pocket.

"Next," another nurse says from my left as that intake window opens.

"Mr. Jenson," I hear my name being called from my right, and I glance over to see who's calling me.

The police officer is gesturing me over to him. I step out of line, losing my place in the hopes he'll have information for me.

"Sir?" I question him.

"Grab Speedy Gonzales over there and follow nurse Kristin here. She'll make sure you get where you need to be for your friend. I hope she makes it through, for you and your daughter's sake. Take care of yourself, and tell your friend to slow her ass down from now on."

"Thank you sir, I will." I walk over and grab Calla. When we make it back to the nurse, the officer is gone.

There's a clicking sound and the heavy wooden door opens right in front of us.

"This way. I'm about to go on break, so I'll take you where you need to go from this direction. Stay close," nurse Kristin instructs as she leads us through the main door and weaves us around the ER into the main hospital. "Your friend is in surgery, so I can't take you directly to her. But I can take you to the surgical waiting room."

"Thank you. Would it also be possible to give me directions to the waiting room so I can text them to my sister? She's bringing my daughter," I inquire as we head down a new corridor.

"No problem. Though it might be easier if you let me type them in. That is, if you don't mind." I pull my phone back out of my pocket and pass it to her once I open my messages with Piper. "I don't mind."

We pass a few other nurses along the way, but for the most part we don't run into many people. I find that a little strange, but we are taking the "authorized personnel only" hallways right now.

"Excuse me, nurse Kristin? Can you also tell us where we might be able to get a DNA test done?" Calla asks, stopping the nurse in her tracks.

She turns to stare at us. "DNA testing? Why do you want to know where to get one of those?" nurse Kristen questions.

"My friend here wants me to verify that the little girl my sister is bringing to the hospital is actually my daughter like Ms. Hartley says she is," I quickly explain.

"Are you two together?" She motions her finger back and forth between me and Calla.

"No!" Calla shakes her head.

"Not in the slightest," I reply at the same time, and we both chuckle. "We're really good friends, and we work together."

"Ah, got ya. More like family, I take it." Nurse Kristen voices that more as a statement than actually asking us a question.

"Yes," we agree.

"Once I get you to the surgical waiting room, I'll give you the directions to the lab. They might be able to get you in while you wait. But don't hold me to that," nurse Kristin adds then resumes walking.

Our trek around the hospital feels like it takes hours when, in reality, it's only minutes. My nerves are shot, and my body is so tense that not even a massage, or sex for that matter, could release the tightness in my muscles. Out of nowhere, Calla grabs my hand, squeezes it, and starts to pull away. Her fingers are barely in my grasp when I glance over at her. Whatever she sees in my face makes her wiggle her fingers until she's holding my hand again. That small act gives me the reassurance I need, and my frayed nerves ease a tiny bit, even if the tension in my muscles doesn't.

Nurse Kristin leads us into a large waiting room. Only a few people are sitting in chairs off to the far side of the room.

"Have a seat, and I'll let the nurses know you're out here," she directs. Calla and I do as she says and take seats close to one of the windows.

My focus goes to my phone. I have a small signal, so I hit 'send' on the message with directions nurse Kristin gave me for Piper.

Within minutes, my phone is ringing. "Hey. Ella and I are

just walking into the hospital. I'll double check which entrance I just entered, but I think we're in the right area from these directions you sent. Thanks, by the way."

"Thank God! I was getting worried. See you shortly," I tell her, and we disconnect.

"Piper's here with Ella I take it?" Calla inquires, sitting back in her chair.

"She is. Do you want to head back to Belladonna?" I'm trying to gauge what her thoughts are.

Calla scrunches her nose. "Fuck no! I'm staying here with you. I get that Piper is your sister, but she's going to help your daughter with this meeting. You need someone here for you, even if it's me just going to get food or something."

"You are fucking amazing you know that? Torrance was a damn idiot for cheating on you. I hope one of these days you find a man that will treat you the way you deserve to be treated. And if I didn't love you like a sister, I'd try to be that man." I lean in and kiss the side of her head. "Thank you for being here and for staying."

Calla shoulder-bumps me, and a little more tension abates.

"Mr. Jenson?" A lady behind the glass partition calls my name.

I push off the chair and make my way over to her.

"Yes ma'am?"

"I'll make sure the doctor and surgical nurse know you're here. As soon as they can let you know how Ms. Hartley is doing, they will. There's one slight issue. Since you're not family, they might not give you an update," the lady informs me.

"I understand. Our daughter is on her way up now, but she's only seven. I can't let her be alone when she's being told news about her mother," I respond.

"Agreed. We'll get it all worked out."

"Thank you." I turn to head back to my seat when my sister and the most beautiful little girl walk into the waiting room.

My breath catches as I get my first look at my daughter. Her long hair is the same butter pecan shade as Piper's and Hallie's. Piper isn't paying attention, as she's speaking with Ella, so I have a moment to study Ella even though I can't see her whole face.

"Aunt Piper what happened? What's wrong with Mom?" my little girl asks, and my heart just about breaks.

This is not how I fucking wanted to meet my daughter.

CHAPTER 5

Ella

My day has been really, really bad. Earlier, all I wanted was to meet my dad. Now I'm in a hospital waiting room wondering what happened to my mom. And if Aunt Piper is here, when I know she should be in Houston for practice, I know this is going to be bad.

This is going to be really, really bad.

"Piper," a man's deep voice says from behind us.

Aunt Piper drops my hand and runs to the man. I've only ever see the man in pictures Aunt Piper has shown me. *My dad is in the same room as me. I can touch him. Holy crap!* It feels like my feet are stuck in place, and my tummy is doing somersaults. Maybe I should have eaten one of the donuts before we came in, after all.

"Ella, Sweetheart, can you come over here please?" Aunt Piper asks. I shake my head no. "I'm scared," I tell her softly.

My dad slowly walks to me with Aunt Piper by his side. "It's okay Ella," he comforts me as he lowers to his knees. "I'm scared, too."

"Ella, this is your father, Forest. Forest, this is your beautiful daughter, Isabella," Aunt Piper introduces us.

My dad holds his hand out to me. "It's very nice to meet you Ella. I'm sorry we haven't had the chance to meet before now. I was planning on setting up a meeting this week with you and your mom."

"Mom told me she was going to meet with you today. I'd wanted to skip school so I could meet you," I squeak out.

He chuckles. "Well, that would have been an even bigger shock. I'm glad you were at school, though. I wasn't very diplomatic with your mom this morning."

"Aunt Piper warned Mom you'd be pissed off." I quickly cover my mouth.

"Ella!" Aunt Piper bites out.

This time he full-out laughs. "Yes, Piper was right. I'll let you in on a secret. She's not off the hook, either." He gestures at Aunt Piper. "Why don't we go sit with my friend over there and wait for news? Sound like a plan?"

"Yes." The three of us walk over to a pretty dark-haired woman sitting next to a window.

My dad turns to my aunt and says, "Piper, you might remember my friend, Calla." Aunt Piper nods and shakes the woman's hand. "Ella, Calla is my friend and coworker. She owns Belladonna, the restaurant where I work," my dad tells me.

"Hi Miss Calla." I shake her hand and take a seat one space down from her.

"Hi Ella. Piper." Miss Calla nods at each of us, watching my dad, Aunt Piper, and me.

"Are you two dating?" Aunt Piper asks as she sits next to me.

Miss Calla starts to cough.

Dad's eyebrows furrow. "No, Calla was the only one that could come with me and there not be any blood shed. Plus, Nessa hadn't even arrived at Belladonna when I left, and trust me, you don't want Adam here."

"Nessa's going to be livid isn't she?" Aunt Piper asks.

"What do you think?" my dad responds, taking the seat between me and Miss Calla.

"Aunt Piper, can I have one of the donuts you brought?" I look back and forth between my aunt and my dad.

"Sure Sweetheart." She pulls out a rectangular white cardboard box from her bag.

Lifting the lid, I peer in. Aunt Piper brought an assortment of our favorite donuts. I pick one of the glazed ones and take a bite.

The fluffy, sugary donut tastes amazing. This is pure

happiness in a little round treat. I've missed the weekend donut runs with Mom. Swallowing my bite, I face Aunt Piper.

"Hey Aunt Piper? Why did you bring donuts from our favorite donut shop?"

"This morning after your mom met with Forest, she called and told me she wanted me here this week to help when you and your dad would meet. I offered to bring donuts up since your mom said y'all hadn't found a place here yet for your weekly fix. The three of us were going find one this weekend." Aunt Piper's small smile is not quite brightening her face.

"So you were already driving up here today?" I take another bite.

"Yep. As soon as I finished practice, I started my drive. I was going to stay until Sunday afternoon," she responds, holding the box out to my dad and his friend, Calla, who has stayed quiet on his other side.

Forest

SHIT. Piper drove up to help Hallie, and most especially Ella, meet me. I haven't even had a chance to get over my shock of learning I have a daughter. Hallie and Piper were planning for me to see Ella one day this week. My mind is still reeling with these facts.

Waiting for news on Hallie is nerve-racking. With Ella here, I can't ask Piper everything I want to. Though from the looks she gives me, she knows a long-overdue discussion is coming. Ella's homework is spread out on the floor as she diligently works on finishing. I'm a little shocked she has homework already. I'd thought school just started.

A man in scrubs ventures toward our little group as we're the only people who remain in the waiting room.

"Mr. Jenson? I'm doctor Scott. I am the primary surgeon on Ms. Hartley's case." The doctor pauses and glances down at Ella, who's now sitting up watching him closely.

"Hey Ella? Will you walk with me to get something to drink?" Calla sits forward, holding out a hand as she speaks to my daughter.

"I want…" Ella starts to say, tears glistening in her eyes. "Yes, ma'am." She reaches for Calla's hand, wiping one eye.

"Thank you," I mouth to her.

With her free hand, Calla squeezes my shoulder and walks my daughter away. Doctor Scott watches as my friend leads Ella out of earshot.

"In the documentation the police found with Ms. Hartley, she listed you as her 'in case of emergency' contact, along with a Miss Piper Jenson."

"I'm Piper," my sister speaks up.

"As I'm sure you both know, Ms. Hartley was already very sick. Because of her illness, all we are able to do for Ms. Hartley is stabilize her enough so her family can say goodbye. She's on life support and probably won't make it through the night. There's a DNR on file for her. As soon as Ms. Hartley's settled in ICU, one of the nurses will be down to take you to her room."

"DNR? What is that, and what does it mean?" I interrogate the surgeon, not understanding all of his medical alphabet soup.

"It's a 'Do Not Resuscitate' order in her record that she had signed previously. It means that if her heart or other organs give out or shut down, we won't attempt to bring her back. We have to let her go."

Piper gasps at this devastating news, and I have to grab for her quickly and hold her upright as she begins to collapse to the floor. I stabilize Piper and refocus on the doctor.

"Thank you, Dr. Scott. When my daughter gets back we'll want to spend as much time with Hallie as possible," I inform him as I'm attempting to gather the scattered pieces of my heart and soul from that huge emotional bomb he just dropped on us.

As Dr. Scott briskly strides out of the waiting room, I pull my sister into my arms, letting her sob on my shoulder. No matter how pissed I am at her for not telling me about Ella, I can't help but comfort her. She's still my little sister, and she's hurting. While I want to kick her ass, I understand that Hallie, her sorority sister and best friend, is like family to her. Hell, considering our age difference, I see why she feels closer to Hallie than to Nessa or myself. Tonight, I only need to think about her and my daughter.

They need to grieve, and for better or worse, I have to be their rock.

I can't lose my daughter, and Piper is the only person in my family that can help me protect Ella. She's also the only one who can help me bridge the years I've missed. Plus, Mom might kill me if I actually hurt my baby sister.

Piper wipes her tears before stepping away from me to clean up Ella's school work. I move to join her, but she holds up a hand to stop me.

"Let me do this. It will keep my mind on something other than losing my best friend." She sniffles. "I knew this day was coming, but I thought I'd prepared myself better than this." Piper plops onto the floor, more tears billowing in her eyes.

"Piper, I'm sorry you're losing your best friend. I can't imagine..." my words cut off. Piper knows I have no fucking clue how she's feeling right now, and I don't need to try to explain it. "While I am still pissed that you didn't tell me about Ella, I'm not going to push you away. We will have words, but now isn't the time for that. My daughter needs you. She needs someone stable in her life, someone she's known all her life, as we move forward. And like it or not, you are family, and I do love you." I squat down next to her and hand over Ella's books, folders, and papers.

Piper stares at me, wiping away more tears. "I love you, too. And thanks for not pushing me away. You have every right to. When this is all over, I'll take any punishment you want to give." She reaches for me and tries to push me over.

"Aunt Piper?" My daughter's voice is tentative behind me.

"Sweetheart, your dad and I need to talk to you," my sister tells my sweet little girl, and my heart wants to break in two.

"Mommy didn't make it did she?" Ella asks, her lip trembling and tears filling her eyes.

I grab her hand and pull her tiny body into me. "Baby girl, she's still with us. But not for long, I'm afraid. The doctor says we need to say our goodbyes." She wraps her arms around me. "How about I carry you as we go see your mom?"

"Yes please, Daddy," Ella's voice quivers. "Is it okay that I call you that?" Tears stream down her face as she asks, and I wrap her even tighter in my arms.

"Yes baby. And as soon as I'm able, we will make it official. First, lets make sure your mom gets to hold you one last time." Ella lays her head on my shoulder as I pick her up and stand. She locks her ankles around my hips once I'm upright.

Calla steps closer, side hugging me and rubbing Ella's back. "Remember what I said Ella."

Ella nods, and Calla steps away from me.

"I'm going to go get everyone some food and let the guys know what's going on. I'll be back in an hour. Text me with what room you're in."

"Thanks Calla," I reply and start to head for the counter.

"It's what families are for. You know that," she responds and helps Piper off the ground.

"Mr. Jenson, Dr. Scott wanted me to inform you that Ms. Hartley is on the fifth floor. They said she'd be in room 501, but that may have changed once they got her up there," the sweet lady behind the desk informs us.

"Thank you. We'll head up there now." With my daughter in my arms and my sister by my side, we move to the elevator and prepare for our lives to be turned upside down.

CHAPTER 6

Forest

The last few days have been a living hell. Thank God Hallie had everything worked out for when the cancer took her from Ella. If she hadn't had the forethought to take care of so many things, I don't know what I'd have done. It's been five days since Hallie passed, and besides finalizing all her wishes, I've gotten the DNA test, and now we're waiting on the results. Once Piper explained everything to Nessa and our parents, and pulled out her own DNA test results that she'd had done a few years back to help make a case that I was, in fact, Ella's father, the outright name-calling and fighting stopped. At least within hearing distance of Ella.

As soon as my parents saw my daughter, they welcomed

her into the family unconditionally, as did Nessa. Though she still shoots Piper the evil eye on occasion and has a few choice words to say. Her niece has proven she's a Jenson too, as she shoots the evil eye back at her Aunt Nessa. The expression Ella gives is the same one I've seen cross both Nessa and Piper's faces, along with my mother's. She's having no problems fitting right in.

So far, today has been a complete blur, and I'm so glad I have family and friends that want to help. I haven't let Ella out of my sight since Hallie died, so she's missed a few days of school. Thankfully, the school has been extremely under-standing. Turns out Ella's teacher, Ms. Scott, is married to Dr. Scott, so she's been sending me Ella's homework.

Ella has gone to Belladonna with me twice, and everyone there loves her. I think Calla wants to keep her. Ella seems to brighten Calla's mood, and she's been able to make some delicious meals for us. Though she hasn't tried anything new or difficult yet.

Maybe all Calla has needed was something to kick start her mojo. I don't mind if Ella is the one to help.

I've even seen a change in Wes, thank fuck for that. I've wondered when he'd finally pull his head out of his ass.

"Mr. Jenson? It's time," the attendant calls.

Nudging Ella, she pulls my earbuds out of her ears, looking up at me with tears filling her eyes.

Getting to my feet, I straighten my pants and hold my hand out to her. "Let's go baby girl. We need to pay our respects to you mom."

Her bottom lip trembles. "Okay, Daddy."

I love that she already calls me Daddy. There hasn't been a time since we met that she hasn't. Once this is over, I'll need to thank Piper for that, as well. I know she's the one that told Ella all about me.

Once Ella puts my phone in her tiny purse and neatly wraps the headphones so they fit inside it too, she grabs my hand, and we walk into the viewing room the funeral home set up for Hallie. The room is filled with all different types and colors of flowers, with a few plants thrown in. Ella's fingers tighten around my hand, and I know I'll do everything I can to protect her. I glance down at her to see her sweet little face fighting back tears the best she can.

I sink down on one knee in front of her. "Ella, Sweetheart, are you sure you want to do this? We can wait. And if you don't want to wait, it's really okay to cry."

"I want to see Mommy, and I want to be a big girl, too. But Daddy, I do want to cry." She steps into my arms and does just that.

"It's okay to cry baby girl. No one's going to say anything. In fact, you'll see a lot of people crying today and tomorrow," I tell her into her hair, wrapping my arms around her slight body.

"You're not crying Daddy?" Ella pulls slightly back from me.

"I didn't know your mom well, Sweetheart, and I'm being strong for you. It's my job to be strong for you, and it will always be my job, even when I'm really old and gray. If

I would've known about you as a baby, I would've been strong for you then too." Tears continue to stream down her cute face. "Let's go see your mom. I'll be right by your side."

Ella steps back, but I pull her close to me, picking her up as I stand. We make the long walk to the casket and hover there until voices can be heard outside.

"Do you want a minute with your mom alone?" Ella nods, and I put her down. "Let me get the stool for you."

She sniffles and wipes her eyes and nose with the back of her hand. I take a few steps away from the casket and grab the footstool and Kleenex. When I move back to Ella, I pass the tissue to her before placing the stool in the ideal spot for her to stand on.

"Thanks, Daddy." She leans into me for a side hug, and I kiss the top of her head, letting my lips rest there for a moment.

"I'm going to go wait right over there." I gesture to a spot behind her, and she turns to look. "Just call me if you need me."

I walk away, letting Ella have as much time with her mom as possible. Before I know it, more family members are entering the room, but Ella doesn't move. She remains at her mother's side, proving just how strong she really is.

As friends and family make their way to Hallie's casket, Ella comes over to me, taking my hand. She tugs twice, and I bend down to her level.

"Yes, baby girl?"

"Thanks, Daddy." I wipe the tears from her cheeks and haul her into my arms.

"Anytime, Sweetheart." I kiss her cheek and squeeze her tight, and she returns the gesture.

"Now, do you want me to hold you or let you stand so you can greet your Mom's friends and family?" I question, making eye contact with her.

"Will you stay next to me the whole time?" There's a quiver in her young voice, and a trembling lip too.

"I won't leave your side," I assure her.

"Then I'll stand and hold your hand. You're sure that's okay?" She gauges my reaction. I get that she's still unsure of me, not to mention she just lost her mom, and she's off kilter.

"Deal." I kiss the top of her head and stand. She quickly grabs my hand, and we greet my parents together.

Piper follows behind my parents, with Nessa and Adam bringing up the rear. After my family, everyone from Belladonna's kitchen comes to give Ella their condolences. She's truly making a wonderful impression on my friends and co-workers, and each and every one of them gives her their respect when they stop and hug her.

The rest of the line is filled with Hallie's friends and estranged family, I learn, as Ella greets them and introduces me. About three hours in, I'm beat to hell, and I can only imagine what toll this day is taking on Ella. Suddenly, her little body straightens, and there's this new energy about her. To her right stands a group of kids whispering, probably trying not to get in trouble. Behind them are more football players, and by the looks the players are giving the kids, I'd venture to guess the kids belong to them. And I think I spot Calla's brother, Ben, mixed in with this crowd.

I thought he played for a different team? I wonder why Calla didn't say anything about him being in town. Normally we talk about it in the kitchen. Though every time Ben comes in, Wes gets in a mood. Fucker just needs to tell Calla he's into her and take the beat-down Ben will give him like a man.

"Daddy," Ella says pulling my hand, and I squat to her level. "These are my friends from back home. Devin, Chad, Jacob, Davan, Reagan, Ezra, and Serena. Y'all, this is my dad." Her voice has a hint of excitement to it, and I'm not sure if it's from seeing her friends or finally telling people she has a dad.

"It's nice to meet you, sir," the kids repeat, one after another, some almost talking over the others.

All seven of them huddle around Ella, forcing me to let her hand go so they can engulf her in a group hug. I rise as they comfort my girl.

My girl. I'm not sure I'll ever want to stop saying that.

"Come on kids. Let's let Ella finish greeting all these people. Tomorrow y'all can cheer her up," one of the biggest guys I've ever seen tells them. Then he bends down and picks her up in a bear hug.

"Uncle Chris, it's okay." Ella holds the man tight.

God can my little girl be any stronger? She's comforting this huge football player when all he wants to do is comfort her.

Chris puts her back on her feet and holds out a hand to me.

"Forest, right?" He's waiting for me to shake his hand.

I nod, taking his hand with my free one.

"Piper told us a lot about you, especially when Hallie said she was going to finally tell you about Ella. On behalf of myself and the team, I want to say thank you for being here for Ella. We know it can't be easy finding out you have a child seven years later. I know we don't know you, but seeing you here with Ella, you seem like a real stand-up guy. If y'all need anything let us know, and if possible, could you bring her down every once in a while so we can see her?"

"I'm just glad I have her in my life now. Of course I'll bring her down. Or maybe her and Piper can have a girls' weekend once a month when Piper heads back," I reply, and it seems to satisfy him and the guys behind him.

After Chris, the line moves pretty much the same way for the rest of the viewing. By 8:30 PM Ella is about to pass out standing up, so we head to my place, grabbing dinner on the way. We eat, and she is out as soon as she finishes her tacos.

CHAPTER 7

Forest

This morning is already hell, and Ella isn't even up yet. Sitting on the edge of my bed watching her sleep, I feel a bit like a perv. Hopefully, as I get used to having a daughter and someone other than myself to take care of, it won't freak me out quite so much. Though, today I'm not sure if I'm feeling this way because of the fact that I have a daughter sleeping in my bed, or the fact that we have to bury her mother.

Yesterday she was so strong. I'm worried that as we put her mom in the ground, she won't be able to hold herself together like she did at the funeral home. I know I wouldn't be able to keep it together if it was my mom, but maybe this sweet little girl is braver than I am.

"Daddy!" she calls out from her sleep. I scoot closer to her.

"Shhh, I'm here." I lower my head and whisper in her ear as I gently stroke her long hair.

Her eyes open, and she stares at me for a long moment. "Daddy, I don't know if I can do this today. Last night was so hard. All I wanted to do was cry the whole time. After today, I'll never see Mommy again."

Well fuck me.

I pull her out of bed and onto my lap, wrapping my arms tightly around her. "Listen to me. We'll go visit Mommy whenever you want. And even if I'm stuck at Belladonna and you want to go, we'll make arrangements for that to happen. Gramps or Nonna will take you if no one else is able to. Okay?"

Her little body shakes in my arms as she cries, my shirt sleeve soaking up the tears. She's breaking me, and I honestly don't think I can fix any of this.

"I know what I'm about to say isn't going to make things any better, and I realize it was something you did with your mom. But how about you get dressed, and before we go say our final goodbyes, we'll grab some donuts from this great place I know that's close to Belladonna? It's called Voodoo Doughnut, and they make some freaking crazy donuts. Sound good?" I kiss her forehead.

Ella pulls away from me slightly and studies me. "Can we also get one for Mommy? I can put it in the casket."

With those words I finally break, and I shed my first tears for Hallie. "Baby girl, we can do whatever you want to do. If you want to get a dozen donuts for your mom, we will." I pull her back to me and hug her once more.

"Daddy, one is plenty for Mommy. But I want a dozen just for me," she declares into my shoulder.

I chuckle.

"We can get a dozen, but you're only eating two this morning. I'll let you have more later. Like maybe after lunch or dinner. Speaking of, I think Calla said Belladonna was going to have something special for you tonight if you want to eat there."

"Daddy, are you dating Ms. Calla?" Ella starts to move to get dressed, and I notice she's moving a little quicker now that she knows she's getting donuts.

"No, Sweetheart. Calla's just a really great friend. She's been having a hard year and hasn't been herself, so she's excited to help with you. I think helping you takes her mind off what's going on with her." I ruffle her hair.

"Daddy, one last question for now?" I nod. "Is Ms. Calla dating Mr. Wes?"

I chuckle and smile at her. "No, she's not. I'll tell you a secret, though... They both like each other a lot, but they won't get their shit together and date."

"If you're not going to date Ms. Calla then Mr. Wes definitely needs to get his shit together," she pronounces and quickly slaps a hand over her mouth.

All I can do is laugh. I can't scold her for cursing when I just did it in front of her, and she pretty much has a point. I'd really love to say Wes needs to get his head out of his ass, but I can't go there. One curse word is good enough for today.

I'm going to need to watch what I say from now on. Fuck, fuck, fuck. This is not going to be easy.

"Alright young lady, let's not say that word often. Now go get your shower, so we can head to the donut shop."

She scurries off, and soon I hear the water running in the bathroom. While she's getting ready, I get dressed and text the Belladonna crew.

Me: Today is going to fucking suck for Ella. Before we go back to the funeral home I'm stopping by Voodoo. Ella and Hallie would get donuts every weekend, so without us taking donuts to the grave every weekend, this is her last time having donuts with her mom. Do you guys want anything?

Calla: Fuck Forest! Now I want to cuddle her even more. I would say grab me a Cock-n-Balls but you have Ella, so will you get me the Portland Cream?

Wes: You don't need a Cock-n-Balls, you have all of us. Lol. Dude, I'll take a Maple Bacon Bar. Thanks.

Calla: Fuck off Wes.

Me: I can't be laughing right now. Fuckers.

Trey: I can't believe you just went there! Seriously? I'll take a Voodoo Doll. I'll name it Wes for all of us. Then I'll just stick the pretzel in it a few times, and maybe it will help keep the dumbass in line.

Adam: I'm fucking glad Nessa isn't paying attention to her phone. I'm not sure she could handle your shit right now. Forest, we'll take two glazed donuts. Oh shit! She's reading the text! Now we're fucked.

Nessa: What the hell?! We have a funeral to go to! Can't you be adults for a change? How's Ella doing? Do you need anything from us?

Me: Okay I have everyone's orders. Ella is doing as well as can be expected. Calla, I did tell her you'd talked about dinner at Belladonna tonight and that, along with the donuts, put a smile on her face. I just want to double check that we can still do that.

Calla: Hell yes. We've talked about inviting everyone back to Belladonna after the graveside service. Do you want that, or just y'all and the family?

Me: Do we have enough for the football team?

Wes: Probably. We put a notice on the door saying Belladonna was closed today for a private event for the staff, so we should be covered.

Me: Holy shit! Really? This is why y'all are family too. Thank you. I can't tell you how much I appreciate this. I know this hasn't been easy on anyone as I learn this new role as a dad, but the fact that y'all have taken Ella in as one of the family is so fucking amazing. Truly, thank you. Unlike Nessa and Adam, the rest of y'all didn't have to do it.

Wes: I think I speak for everyone now. She is a badass little girl, and while we haven't known her long, she's yours, so she's ours. Whether she likes it or not, she has two more uncles and an aunt here for her. Granted, Uncle Wes will be more beneficial when she's older. Lol

Calla: You're such an ass. And except for the last part, I agree.

The door to the bathroom opens, and as I glance over at my little girl dressed in black, my heart shatters for her. At her age, she shouldn't have to deal with something so devastating.

"Daddy can you help me with the zipper, please?" she requests in a soft voice. "And possibly my hair?"

I gesture for her to come over to me, and I take a seat on the bed again. "Let me finish this text, and I'll see what we can do."

Me: Okay, Ella's about ready. We'll see you after we get the donuts. Nessa, I may need your help with her hair when we get to the funeral home.

I drop the phone on the bed and zip her dress. "Okay. I'll be honest... I don't know much about girls' hair, so I've asked Aunt Nessa to help fix yours when we get to the funeral home if I can't get it right. Or you can ask Aunt Calla, or Aunt Piper."

"*Aunt* Calla?" She spins around, eyes wide and staring at me.

"Yep. I was just texting with Calla, Trey, Wes, Uncle Adam, and Aunt Nessa. We have a group chat since we're always hanging out, and Wes says you've gained two more uncles and an aunt. So your family has grown a bit more than you thought." I reach for her hands and hold them, squeezing slightly.

More tears billow in her eyes. Those tears fucking gut me every time I see them. And while I know it's going to take time for her to be happy, I can't wait for that day. This level of sadness is one of the hardest things I have ever had to helplessly watch on such a sweet face.

CHAPTER 8

Forest

We pull into the employee parking lot behind Belladonna and park in the first space. I gesture for Ella to wait as I jump out of the truck and walk around to help her out. If she gets her dress dirty before the service, I doubt I'll hear the end of it from the women in my family. With Ella's hand in mine, I close the door behind her and lock it as we head for 6th Street. The walk to Voodoo Doughnut takes a little longer than usual as I have to slow my pace for Ella.

"I guess I should've parked closer for us. Sorry, Sweetheart." I squeeze her hand as we stroll down the street.

"It's okay Daddy. I'm kinda happy it's going to take longer. I'm really not ready to see Mommy yet." She's somehow managing to keep her tears at bay for the time being.

Tough little girl. And she's all mine.

We make it to the donut shop and, thankfully, the place is slow. If we had come in during peak times, I don't know when we'd finally get out.

"Go see what you want. I need to place everyone else's order," I tell her, and she quickly heads to the display counter.

That's the fastest I've seen her move since I met her. I chuckle.

"Daddy, why is there a donut called Cock-n-Balls?" Ella asks, looking over her shoulder at me.

Fuck me. My eyes close, and I really do try to hold in my laughter, but I just can't. Hearing her sweet little voice say 'cock-n-balls' is more than I can take, and I'm so fucking glad Wes isn't with us to witness that. He would never let me hear the end of it if he was.

"How about you ask Uncle Wes when you give it to him? Make sure you ask him in front of Aunt Calla and Uncle Trey. I bet they'll want to take a picture of his face." *Did I really just tell my daughter to ask Wes that? Shit, I'm so fucked!*

Stepping up to the register, I glance at the donuts and quickly decide what I'm going to get while Ella is still studying the huge variety of donuts they offer.

"Forest Jenson, right?" the woman behind the counter asks me.

My brows furrow as I stare at her. She doesn't look familiar, but that doesn't mean I haven't hooked up with her sometime in the past. There have been a few crazy nights when I've been out with Trey, Wes, and our friend Rex. Even then I can normally place the face. Not with this gorgeous woman, though.

"Yes," I answer hesitantly. "I'm sorry... have we met?" I inquire, still trying to figure out if I know her but coming up completely blank.

"Sorry, no," she answers and shakes her head slightly then smiles shyly as her cheeks turn a cute shade of pink. "But I know Trey and Calla from Belladonna, and they come in here on occasion. To help speed things along, Trey already called in the order for everyone but you and... Ella, right?"

"That's me!" my daughter pipes up happily, smiling at the woman.

My daughter's smile is amazing, and I'm so fucking pissed I've never seen it until now. It could light up a room, and *holy fuck* I'm going to need a bat and a gun to keep the fucking boys away from this sweet girl. *I'm seriously fucked! It's a good thing Wes and Trey have an arsenal. We're going to need it. And sooner rather than later, too.*

"She's a cutie. But I didn't think any of the main staff at Belladonna had kiddos," the woman remarks, biting her bottom lip. That's when I notice it's pretty fucking sexy the way she bites it and smiles, her eyes sparkling.

She is dressed in a white tank that shows off her perky breasts that are possibly a C-cup but, I can't be sure. I'm not as good as Rex when it comes to guessing women's cup sizes. They would fit in the palm of my hand, that I am sure of. Her hair, even pulled back in a ponytail, is the shade of milk chocolate when the light hits it just right.

Shit... I can't be thinking like this with my daughter in the room. Today has to be all about her. I'm such an asshole.

I snap out of my musings regarding the woman just in time to here Ella ask, "Can I have one of these please, miss? And one of those? I need to give one to my mom." The woman's smile fades slightly as she moves to take Ella's donuts out of the display counter.

"And for you?" She looks at me, her voice a little less friendly.

"Apple fritter and a glazed please. Ella did you only want one donut?" I smile down at her.

"Sorry, Daddy. I'm so used to only being able to get one that I forgot you said I could have two. If I get two, can we get another one for Mommy to put with her?" Ella's lips tremble a bit as she speaks.

I drop down on one knee so I'm eye level with her. "Sweetheart, I wasn't kidding earlier when I said I would put as many donuts in your mom's casket as you want. I'd prefer that we eat them if we get her more than two, but whatever you want to do, I'll do it for you." I pull her in for a hug, and she sighs against me.

"Miss can I-" Ella starts to say when the lady cuts her off.

"How about you call me Jax? It's what my friends call me," Jax tells Ella, making my little girl smile again.

"Thanks, Jax. Why do your friends call you that? And can you add a chocolate one? I'll let you pick which chocolate, and I'd like to add the vi-sc-ous hib-isc-us," Ella sounds out the words. "It looks pretty, and I think Mommy would have liked it." Ella's smile falls as her expression turns downcast once more.

"Would have?" Jax questions.

I gently place my hand on Ella's shoulder. "Her mom just passed away, so two of the donuts will be placed in the casket with her. Sorry," I wince as I explain.

"I'm so sorry for your loss. Both of you," Jax says, grabbing the other donuts.

"Daddy didn't really lose anyone. He just gained me," Ella tells her, still looking down.

Jax's brows raise at Ella's pronouncement.

"Sorry. Our story is a little strange, and today is a shitty day all around," I add.

"No worries." Jax finishes packaging up the donuts then walks around the counter and kneels in front of Ella.

"My friends call me Jax because I didn't like Jackie as a nickname. And sometimes Jaclyn is just a little too formal for me. Now I have a question for you," Jax states, and Ella lifts her head so she can see her better.

"I lost my mom when I was a few years older than you, so I know this isn't easy. Can I give you a hug?" Jax places the box of donuts on the ground next to her and holds her arms open.

Ella glances at me then back at Jax and steps in to hug her.

"Maybe sometime you can tell me about your mommy?"

Ella speaks so softly it's hard to hear her as she continues. "That is, if I can talk Daddy into coming back here. Getting donuts was something I did with my Mommy every weekend. It's why we're doing it today, so I can have one more donut day with her." That explanation broke whatever dam had been holding Ella's tears at bay, and she lets them loose. When Jax glances up at me, it looks as if tears are filling her eyes as well, and she grabs my daughter in a tight hug one more time.

"You're so lucky to have a daddy who's able to do that for you. You watch out for him." Jax winks at me as she gives Ella the insight of someone who knows heartbreak the same way she does.

It hurts my heart, but also makes me want to get to know this woman. Even if we only end up as friends, she is someone that can help my daughter in a way not many people are able to. I had been thinking of talking to Calla, but maybe she and Jax, if they really are friends, can have a girl's lunch with Ella and begin to help her through this in a way that I can't since I've never lost anyone close to me.

Picking up the box, Jax rises and passes it to me. "Here you go. Why don't you guys stop in this weekend if you're up for it? I'll buy you a doughnut and something to drink."

"Can we, Daddy? I know we need to do something just for us but--" the tears are still streaming down Ella's cheeks.

"Baby girl, we have plenty of time to do something for us. If you need donuts once a week for a while, we'll do it. But if we do, we split the donuts. Deal?" I hold out my hand for her, but all she does is shake it.

"Deal. Thanks, Miss Jax. See you this weekend," Ella says, her voice still somber as she walks toward the door.

"Maybe your 'thing' becomes making doughnuts together. Does she know you're the pastry chef at Belladonna?" Jax wants to know as she's taking my outstretched hand and shaking it.

"She does. But I hadn't thought about baking donuts with her. Maybe when we come in this weekend you can give me some ideas so we can make that our 'thing.'" Jax lets my hand go.

"Deal. See you soon, Forest."

"Soon," I repeat to myself as I follow my daughter to the front door where she's patiently waiting.

CHAPTER 9

Jax

I thought for sure this week was going to drag ass, especially after I suggested Forest and Ella come back by the shop. *What the hell was I thinking? He just lost the girl's mother!* Yet, he didn't seem as torn up as some people are when they lose their spouse. Hell, my father couldn't function for years after my mom died from the brain tumor. *Ella did make the comment that Forest gained her, so maybe they were divorced. Stop over-analyzing.* Thank God I am in the back today. I'm not sure I could keep my head on straight if I was working with the customers. I'd probably get all the orders wrong.

"Shit!" I say a little too loudly, and the other four bakers glance at me over their shoulders. Brad, one of the few weekend employees, pops his head in. Everyone else in the kitchen gets back to baking.

"Jax, you okay back here?" he calls out.

"Yeah, I just got dough all over me." I roll my eyes, not that anyone can see me do it, but it makes me feel better.

"Do you need any help? It's slowed down a bit," he offers with a twinkle in his baby blues, a stark contrast to his velvety hazelnut skin tone.

Damn, when that boy gets older he's going to be trouble, but his charms don't work on me. I've known him for way too long. Not to mention that while he says he's nothing like his brother, he truly is when it comes to his appearance. Except those eyes.

Speaking of his brother.

"Bradley get your ass back to the front. Jax doesn't need your help," my business partner, and best friend since childhood, growls as he walks through the back door.

"One of these days she's going to say yes to me," Brad responds and smirks as he walks off.

"Fat chance little brother," CJ mumbles, grabbing a towel on his way over to me.

He has a point. If I were going to date either of them it would be CJ. Hell, it actually *was* CJ once upon a time, but we made better friends than lovers. And while Brad has those striking baby blue eyes, something always drew me to stare at CJ's miss-matched ones. He has one blue and one brown eye, and even after knowing him all these years, I'm still intrigued when I look at them.

"Here you go." He tosses the towel at me. Catching it, I start to clean my arm off as he asks, "So what happened? Normally it's just flour you have all over yourself, not the dough." His smile is huge and maddening, as he can't hold back his mirth.

I just want to punch him. But I won't, because he's like family. *Huh... maybe that's why I should.*

Worrying my bottom lip, I lean against the counter I was working on and drop the towel on the edge. "What happened is I keep thinking about this guy."

"Oooh a guy," he teases.

"Are we twelve again?" I shoulder check him.

CJ chuckles. "No, but when a guy makes you lose focus while you're baking, I'm honor-bound to give you shit. You do it to me all the damn time." He bumps me back.

"Yeah. Yeah."

"So who is he? What did he do to make you act all girly?" he gestures to me and the mess I created while I was daydreaming. "Could I take him out if I needed to? I haven't had to kick anyone's ass for you in years. I might need to practice on Bradley."

Covering my mouth, I try to hold back my laughter. It doesn't work and the smile that accompanies the laugh is big enough to reach my eyes.

"No practicing on your brother. Although, if you keep

calling him Bradley he's going to want to try to take *you* down. Now he wants to be called *Brad*. You know this." CJ waves me off. He likes to fuck with his little brother, as siblings usually do, and since Brad has been trying to one-up CJ at every turn lately, the hassling is what he gets. "As far as this guy is concerned," I continue, "I met him Tuesday morning. His name is Forest, and he's the pastry chef at Belladonna. I only know that because the owner and another chef have been in here a few times."

"Calla, right? And Trey is the one she comes in with?" he confirms, checking the counter before crossing his arms and leaning against it.

"Right. So Tuesday, Trey called in an order for pick up under Forest's name. Forest came in with his little girl. They were off to her mom's funeral. I'm not sure what the dynamic is between them, though. It seemed a little... off, and I can't quite put my finger on why. But his daughter, Ella, was sweet and so incredibly sad." I pause, thinking back to the little girl, and how she let me hug her.

"You felt a connection to her didn't you?" CJ questions me, unfolding his arms and pulling me into a hug. "So is it him? Or her?"

"Honestly? Both. They both pulled on my heart strings, and I can't stop thinking about them." Resting my head on his shoulder, I wait for him to tell me how crazy this sounds.

"So, on the crazy scale, eh... it's about a three, but if you run into him again, who knows what could happen." He kisses the side of my head. "Now get back to baking, so I can work on my geeky stuff," he jokes, using cheesy air quotes, "as you like to call it."

I stick my tongue out at him as he releases me and heads toward the office. Turning to the counter, I get back to work on the doughnuts. Thankfully, my mind doesn't wander as much after telling CJ about Forest and Ella. In fact, I'm able to make several more batches of doughnuts without incident now. It's like I'm supercharged.

"Hey Jax?" Brad calls back to me. "There's someone here to see you." I scan the room to see where everyone is in their baking process. Satisfied everything is moving along like it should be, I head to the front, glancing at my watch as I go. *Shit! Time really has been flying by.*

"Who's here to see me?" I ask Brad once I'm at the display counters.

He gestures across the room to two women and a little girl. His hand comes up to my face, and he brushes something off my cheek.

"You and that flour. I'm not sure how y'all don't have to order more flour than you do. I swear you're always covered in it. Can you take these over there with you please?" He hands me one of our pink boxes and a drink. "I'm going to help the next person in line."

"Sure. Who does the drink go to?" I question as he starts to move away.

"The blonde," he replies and steps up to the counter, taking an order from the next customer.

With a sigh, I amble over to the table. The seating area is

almost full today, which I love seeing. A lot of the time, folks order their doughnuts and go, but it's nice to see when they sit and enjoy them here. With fall classes just starting back up, we'll get more students wanting the sugar high as they study.

"Excuse me... " I say to the table as I arrive. "... y'all needed to speak to me?"

The little girl turns around, and the ladies stop speaking. "Ms. Jax!" Ella exclaims, a small smile on her face. Her eyes are so puffy and red-rimmed that it breaks my heart all over again. It's not easy to lose a mom, but at her young age, I can't even imagine. *And here I thought fourteen was hard enough.*

I place the box on the table before squatting down to her level. "Hey pretty girl. How are you today, Ella?"

She slips out of her chair and hugs me like she's never going to let go.

"Not so good. Daddy had to work for Aunt Calla today for a little bit, and I'm supposed to be doing my homework from the days of school that I've missed, but I can't con-cen-trate," she stammers out the word. "So I asked Daddy if Aunt Nessa and Aunt Calla could bring me down here for a pick me up."

Her explanation fills my heart, and I smile. "Well, hopefully these will help." I gesture to the box. "But wouldn't one of your dad's desserts do the trick?"

She shrugs. "Maybe. But I wanted to visit with you. Also, the other day, Thursday I think, when we were all having lunch before Belladonna opened, we were talking about you."

"Ella," the blonde groans as Calla chuckles.

"She is *just* like Forest. Hi Jax, this is Nessa," Calla nods to her friend. "She is Forest's twin. What Ella is trying to say, in a long-winded and roundabout way, is that she and Forest mentioned you had invited them back here for donuts. Ella informed a small group of us that you'd lost your mom when you were young, and we were wondering if you could kind of give all of us a little guidance?" Calla's expression turns sheepish.

Blowing out a deep breath, I study Ella's face then her aunt's. "Every situation is different.…" I focus on Ella again. There is so much hope shining in her eyes, and I know I can't say no. "If it will help, I'd be happy to talk to whoever wants to listen."

Ella flings her arms around me again and squeezes me tight. "Thanks, Ms. Jax. Daddy really wanted to ask you himself. He thinks you're pretty," Ella whispers in my ear.

How can I refuse this adorable little girl?

"Thank you," Calla says, and Nessa nods. "If you're up for it after your shift, why don't you come down to Belladonna? You can have dinner, and either Forest or I can get something set up. Honestly, it might be all of us asking you questions to help Forest out if he's busy."

"Sure." My head is spinning at this turn of events. The ladies start to gather their box of doughnuts and drinks as my brain restarts. "Can I bring a friend with me?" I blurt out.

"Please do. We realize this is a crazy request. We'd rather you feel as comfortable as possible," Calla says as she moves toward the door.

Ella hugs me one more time, her little frame buzzing with a little more life. "See you soon Ms. Jax!" she tells me before taking both women's hands and walking out.

That little girl might be the death of me. Or... maybe new life?

CHAPTER 10

Forest

Tonight has been a clusterfuck, and there is no way to blame it on Calla's mojo being gone. However, I still wish like hell that it would come the fuck back... like yesterday. Being down a chef sucks, and she's such a great chef. Though, if she'd been cooking today, she wouldn't have been able to run my errand, so maybe it's a small blessing after all. The kitchen door swings open, and Ella flies into the room.

"Daddy, with Jax coming to dinner tonight, can I please stay and sit in the bar area with Uncle Adam while everyone works? I'll do my homework. I don't want to leave with Aunt Piper!" Ella pleads, her bottom lip sticking out in a pout as she crosses her arms over her chest.

Damn I'm in trouble with that look. I fight to hold back my grin. I do understand that I can't encourage this behavior, but it *is* cute, and if it wasn't for the woman strolling back here right now, I'd say no. I stop working on the dessert I really need to finish, moving around my station to pick up my daughter. Furrowing my brows, I stare at my younger sister as tension fills the room. She's damn lucky Nessa hasn't walked back here after her. And whether anyone realizes it or not, in the short amount of time since Ella came into my life, she's become a part of the Belladonna family. There isn't anything these friends of mine wouldn't do for her.

"Piper, what the hell are you doing back here? You're not staff," I growl at her, grinding my molars together.

"Ella took off, so I followed her. Since half the family works here, I figure I can go anywhere I want," Piper snarks as she rolls her eyes.

And this is why I'm still pissed at her. She doesn't get that her actions have consequences. Just one more reason I'm glad Calla took Nessa with her when she offered to go down to Voodoo Doughnuts and talk to Jax with Ella.

"First of all, the staff knows Ella. They don't know you," I remind her as the kitchen door swings open again, and Nessa strides purposefully in, a scowl firmly in place on her face.

"Get the fu... sorry, Ella... hell out of the kitchen, Piper. Ella, Sweetheart, if your dad says yes, Uncle Adam and I will watch over you in the bar area. We'll let you stay in the booth you were in." Nessa moves further into the kitchen.

"She shouldn't been here all the time," Piper frowns at Nessa then me, her hands going straight to her hips like Mom used to do. Mom could pull it off. Piper can *not*.

"Please Daddy? Can I? Just tonight. Monday, after school, if you want me to stay at Nonna and Gramp's house, I will." Ella's eyes are glassy as she pleads with me, and my heart hurts so bad for her. I'm not sure it has stopped hurting for my little girl at any point since Hallie died.

"Okay," I agree. "You've been here all week, anyway. Tonight's not going to hurt anything. That said, you will listen to Aunt Nessa and Uncle Adam. If Aunt Piper stays, you'll listen to her as well. If one of them tells you no, don't ask the others and, under no circumstance, do you come in here because they won't let you have anything. Do I make myself clear?" I insist as I maintain eye contact with her. It's something my father used to do to me when I was a kid. It didn't always work, but for the most part we understood he meant business when he looked at us like that.

Piper huffs. Her rigid posture saying more than any words that might come out of her mouth. What she doesn't realize is... I really don't give a fuck what she thinks right now. Sure she helped raise Ella, so she knows how Hallie handled everything. Yet, the fact that she never told me about my daughter is still a huge issue, and now that Hallie has been laid to rest, we definitely need to have it out. Tonight is not the night, though. And neither is having this fight in front of Ella the right way to handle our issues. She's an innocent in this mess, and right now, I'll do whatever my daughter needs to feel loved and wanted.

"Hallie, wouldn't-" Piper starts, and I glare at her.

Ella's breath hitches at the sound of her mother's name.

"Piper, I'm not having this conversation with you. Especially not right now. You are Ella's aunt, not her mother. Stop and think about your niece instead of yourself. If this is what Ella needs right now then it's what she's going to get." My focus moves back to Ella. "Alright young lady, go out with Aunt Nessa. If I get a minute, I'll come check on you. If you get hungry, let one of them know, but don't chase them around the restaurant," I remind her before kissing her head and setting her back on the ground.

"Yes sir. Thanks, Daddy." She kisses my cheek before walking over to Nessa and grabbing her hand. They quickly exit the kitchen, Piper on their heels after she finishes glaring at me.

Guess she wishes Hallie would've given her custody. Speaking of which, I need to read that damn letter she wrote that her attorney handed to me after the reading of her will. Maybe it will give me a little more insight on why she didn't.

Rounding my prep counter, I pick up where I left off on the dessert and hope the servers don't come back anytime soon. One by one, as I start on the next orders, Calla, Trey, and Wes stop by my area. They don't say anything. They just pat my back or arm as they make their rounds around the kitchen. Calla does take a little extra time to taste whatever batter I'm working on. At least her taste buds didn't go wonky when her cooking did. She still has a palate I would die for. It's one of the reasons she's such a great chef. *Normally.*

As the first round of the dinner rush starts to ebb, the second wave of orders flow in. It's at this time Nessa comes back into the kitchen, a mischievous grin filling every inch of her face.

Oh shit. What did she do? The only time I saw this expression growing up was when I was about to get in trouble because, God forbid, my twin do something devious. It *had* to have been me. Granted, I was normally right there with her. But still, our parents didn't call her out on *anything* we did. It was always me that took the fall. *I can't believe you let your sister do that with you! Forest, why did you take Nessa with you?* Yeah, I'm so going to need to watch what Nessa teaches Ella.

Nessa strolls over to me. "So... you want the good news first, or bad?"

"Neither? I don't know if I can handle more of either this week," I tell her, kneading the dough I'm working.

"Too bad. Mom and Dad are here. They're sitting in the bar with Ella and Piper. Before you ask, yes, Piper is griping about you letting Ella stay here tonight. Mom and Dad gave her *that look.*" She chuckles, and chills run down my spine.

"That laugh is still evil, and you know it. Is that the good news or the bad?" I ask, setting the dough to the side and starting on the next dessert that spits out of the order reader.

She stands there, not saying anything, tapping her finger against her bottom lip. My brow arches at her.

"Jax just arrived. She's with a guy, and they're sitting in the bar in the booth next to Ella," she says and turns to leave.

"Well, fuck. Okay. Uh... let me finish this order, and I'll stop by the tables," I state, letting out a long, deep frustrated breath.

Jax will be one more issue Piper's going to bitch about.

"Forest, I'm pretty sure Jax and the guy she's with are just friends." Nessa grins then laughs. "With how they talk to each other, I'd be shocked if they're on a date. By the way, she's fucking hot. If you get a shot at dating her, take it." And with that pronouncement, she exits the kitchen.

Laughter soon fills the kitchen as I roll my eyes. At least something finally broke the spell Piper created earlier. Granted, I can't throw the blame all on her. We had people call in sick tonight, which threw off the kitchen and the waitstaff, but she sure as fuck didn't help.

Focusing on what I need to finish, I block out everything around me. That is, until the feeling of eyes boring into me send chills running down my spine. Glancing up, I see Wes is standing next to me.

"Dude, where the hell were you just now? I said your name twice." He smirks. "Let me take over for a bit. Go talk to your parents and the chick that's going to help us with Ella."

I run a hand through my hair. "Yeah, okay. Thanks, Wes."

"No problem, man. We're family. It's what we do." Wes steps back and lets me escape my space.

As I'm heading for the door, Calla stops me. She doesn't say a word. She simply takes a towel to my hair and rubs it before taking her hand and fixing whatever she did to it.

"Really? You're cleaning me up?" I ask as I see Trey off to my right shaking his head.

Calla shrugs and steps out of my way, and I leave the kitchen.

I'm never nervous around chicks. But as I make my way toward Jax, I realize my confidence has disappeared.

Fuck.

CHAPTER 11

Ella

Aunt Piper is driving me crazy. I swear, if she doesn't stop being a witch to Daddy, I'm going to scream. The routine she wants me to keep was Mom's. It's not Daddy's, and I need to be on Daddy's routine. *I hope she goes home to Houston soon.*

That is a thought I never thought I'd have. I hope that doesn't make me a bad person. Until this week, I hadn't realized the differences between Aunt Piper and her brother and sister. Sure she'd said they were very different, but I don't think I wanted to believe it. After the episode in the kitchen, and what she's been saying to Nonna and Gramps... yeah, I can see it. Thankfully, they're trying to shut her up.

Keeping my head down, I shift in the booth, pretending

to focus on my homework so the adults around me don't realize my attention is mostly on their conversation.

"He has no right to change the way Hallie and I raised her. She needs to stick to what she knows," Aunt Piper whines between sips of her wine.

"You listen to me, young lady," Nonna fusses at her. "You kept a huge secret from this family. I understand why Hallie wanted to spend all the time she had with Ella. But the fact remains that *you* didn't try to talk Hallie out of that crazy plan, so Ella would already know her other family when something happened to Hallie. And that was selfish." Nonna's expression is pained as she chastises Aunt Piper.

"Mom, she needs--"

"Enough, Piper!" Gramps cuts in. "You will not disrespect this family, nor will you keep up this bitchfest in front of Ella. She's been through enough this week. Act your age."

At Gramps' words, Aunt Piper finally shuts up, and I'm left in shock. Aunt Piper sulks from across the table, and I force my mouth to stay closed even though my jaw wants to drop open. I feel like the old cartoons Mom watched with me where the character's mouth dropped open and their eyes bugged out. In all my seven years, I don't think I've ever had this reaction to something someone has said. *Have I ever had this reaction?*

Movement at the booth next to us catches my attention. One of the voices sounds familiar. Wanting to see if I recognize the person it's attached to, I glance up just in time to see Jax's profile as she takes her seat. For some reason, seeing Jax makes me antsy. I want to slide under the table and go over to her. Besides Daddy, Jax is the only other person I feel completely comfortable with. Even now with Aunt Piper, I'm not fully at ease like I used to be. *Shouldn't I feel more comfortable with Aunt Piper than Daddy or Jax?*

Aunt Nessa stops by our booth shortly, and after our outing with Aunt Calla this afternoon, I don't get why Aunt Piper doesn't get along with her. She's funny and smart, and Aunt Nessa only wants to protect me and Daddy. This afternoon she watched Jax instead of talking. At first I thought she was being rude, but after we left, and Aunt Calla asked her questions, I realized she was sizing her up.

If my understanding is right, Aunt Calla and Aunt Nessa want to do more than just have Jax help Daddy and me through this rough time. They think Daddy and Jax should date. That would be cool. Jax could make donuts with us. Her donuts are *soooo* good. I could eat at Voodoo every morning if Daddy would let me. Lost in my donut thoughts, I don't see the newcomer at our table.

"How's the homework coming baby girl?" Daddy asks. I turn my attention in his direction and scrunch my nose. "That good, huh?" he laughs.

"You actually thought she could do work here?" Aunt Piper gestures at our surroundings.

"Piper," Gramps growls.

"I would have more work completed, but Aunt Piper has been bitching since Nonna and Gramps got here," I tell him then quickly cover my mouth.

"Isabella!" Aunt Piper admonishes me.

Nonna and Gramps must have the same expression I had when Gramps lit into Aunt Piper earlier. Daddy's trying to hold back his laughter, his eyes twinkling as his cheeks redden. Then there's laughter all around us.

Aunt Nessa pops over. "That's my niece! Damn, I'm really going to love hanging with you." She laughs and holds a hand out for a high-five. I smack it. "That said, let's not give Nonna and Gramps here a heart attack, or get your Dad in trouble with your teachers. Sound like a plan?"

Scrunching my nose at the thought of losing Nonna and Gramps, or Daddy getting into trouble, I readily agree. Chuckles sound from the next booth over, the one where Jax and her friend sit, making me smirk. *At least a few adults get me and understand where I'm coming from.*

Jax

Damn, this Piper chick sounds like a bitch. What is her issue?

The waitress steps up to the table. She practically eye fucks CJ before placing his pint of Brewtorium Electric Lederhosen in front of him, which is typical. He *is* hot. Without taking her eyes off him, she puts my whiskey and ginger, with a lime twist, on the table.

"Do you know what you want to order?" She only asks CJ, ignoring me completely.

CJ gestures for me to start as he takes a sip of his drink.

His eyes practically roll back in his head, and he takes a longer pull of the beer.

With a slight shake of my head, and an eye roll to boot, I lift the menu.

"We'd like to start with the roasted brussels sprouts, and I'd like the chicken butternut squash fettuccine alfredo please. Can you tell me what veggies come with it?" I inquire, glancing between the waitress and the menu.

"It doesn't come with veggies," she responds, her attention still on my companion.

I'm not sure if the chick gets that he's not paying the least bit of attention to her. In fact, I don't think he'd be able to tell me her cup size if I asked. *What the hell is he so focused on?*

"Excuse me," I hear a male voice say from the booth next to us. "Sorry to interrupt, but the alfredo comes with broccoli," Forest pipes in, leaning over to correct the server.

"Good grief. I guess we need to set up a training to go over the menu," Nessa quips, and with her standing next to Forest, I can definitely see the family resemblance.

"Sorry Chef, Nessa." The waitress's expression is contrite as she finally takes her eyes off CJ. Forest nods, and his attention, along with Nessa's, returns to their conversation at the booth next to mine. Trying not to smile, I force my mouth to stay closed.

CJ blinks. "She'll take the broccoli. I'd like to try the seafood linguine." He takes the menu from me before handing both of them to the waitress.

"I'll get these right in," she informs us, scurrying off.

"Alright. Spill," I say as I pick up my drink and take my first sip. The burn from the whiskey sliding down my throat is mild compared to what I normally get when I'm out. "Damn! This is either damn good whiskey and mixing it with the ginger was criminal, or the bartender blended it perfect-ly," I comment, staring at the amber liquid.

Nessa stops at the table as she moves away from the booth behind me. "It's both, I promise. I'll let Adam know he has some mad skills behind the bar for you." She winks and saunters off, chuckling as she goes.

"Huh. That seems a bit ominous doesn't it?" CJ muses as he watches her walk away.

"Not sure," I reply and focus on his less than stellar mood.

A snort comes from my right, taking my attention off CJ as Forest steps up to the table. "My sister is married to the bar manager. He's the one that made your drink. I need to head back to the kitchen, but if y'all don't mind hanging out a little while after you eat, I'd like to chat. It's been a crazy night." He gestures with his head toward the booth behind me.

"Sure. We can do that. I feel like having dessert tonight anyway, and I know I can talk his sweet tooth into some." I smile, and CJ nods.

"Great. I'll bring it out when it's finished so we can talk then," he says, and I nod in agreement.

"That works." Forest walks away, and I stare after him, checking out his ass until he's out of view. "Back to my question dude... and no dodging. Tell me what's going through that handsome head of yours," I remark, glaring at him.

CJ sits back against the seat and lets out a long sigh. "It's this girl I've been talking to. She keeps giving off hot and cold vibes, and I'm about done trying." He reaches for his beer again.

"You'll have to give me examples, otherwise I can't help you." I roll my eyes at him, and he smirks back at me.

"Honestly, Jax I'm not sure. Today she blew me off when I tried to talk to her, but a few days ago she acted like she wanted to meet up for drinks this weekend. I know that women like to play hard to get at times, but she takes it to a whole different level," he grumbles before finishing his beer.

"Okay, we need to get you something stronger than beer. And for once, listen to me when I say if she's going to play games like this, she's not worth it. Stay away from her. I mean it. You deserve better, and I'm not just saying that because you're my best friend. I've seen you be an ass before, but you're a great guy, and treating you like that's just shitty." I bump his leg with my foot, but he merely shrugs.

The brussel sprouts arrive before I can add anything more, and we order two more drinks then dig in. The sprouts are mouth-watering, perfectly roasted, and they practically melt in my mouth. Considering the reviews I've been seeing lately on Belladonna, I'm pleasantly surprised and can't wait to try the alfredo.

For the rest of the appetizer and into our meal, we chat

about everything. I don't hear much now from Ella's booth until everyone gets up to leave.

"Night Ms. Jax! Enjoy Daddy's dessert. He's really good at them. Will you be at Voodoo tomorrow? I'd like Daddy and me to stop by if it's okay? Maybe you can show us how to make the doughnuts?" Ella requests as she stops at the table while everyone else keeps walking. *Do they realize she's lagged behind to talk?*

"I'll talk to your Daddy about it. Go catch up with your family, so you don't scare them okay?" I suggest, reaching out to touch her cute face.

She holds still, letting me touch her. "Thanks Ms. Jax."

"Ella, lets go. Leave those nice people alone," the younger one of the women says as she heads back to get Ella. By the sound of her voice, I gather it's the one they called Piper.

"Bye, Ms. Jax." Ella starts for her family as I say my goodbye.

CHAPTER 12

Forest

"Order up!" Calla calls out before strolling over to me. "Hey Forest, I have a set of desserts for you, and it looks like they're heading to Jax's booth. Why don't you take a break once you make them so you can go talk to her? We'll cover anything else that comes in."

"That would be great. After the shit Piper pulled tonight, I really need to talk with Jax," I reply. I'm drained, and I think everyone can tell.

"Dude, I've got you," Wes yells from the grill.

I give him a salute before pulling the ticket for Jax and her friend's request. The creamy cheesecake won't take anytime to plate, but the cast iron baked decadent triple chocolate brownie will. *I'm damn glad I made the ice cream earlier today.*

Pulling out the ingredients, I get to work making the small brownie. Plating then adding the garnishes is a breeze, and within five minutes after the brownie finishes baking, I'm heading for Jax's booth. Their server tries to stop me, but I bypass her and keep moving toward the bar.

"Hey Forest, you want me to make you a drink?" Adam calls from behind the bar as I stroll by him.

"Please," I answer with a nod.

Stepping up to the booth I ask, "Who ordered the cheesecake, and who ordered the brownie?"

"Just place them in the center of the table. We always share when we order dessert," Jax states, moving plates and drinks out of the way for the new dishes.

"Here you go, man." Adam pushes a highball glass into my hand as I turn toward him.

"Thanks. It's been one of those days," I mutter.

"Considering the family was here... yeah, I know," Adam adds as he walks away.

"May I sit with y'all so we can talk, and you can enjoy those?" I gesture to the desserts.

"Definitely," Jax pronounces, scooting over to make room for me. "Forest, this is my best friend and business partner, CJ Steele."

"It's nice to meet you, CJ. Thanks for coming out with Jax for this conversation." I hold out my hand to him.

He shakes it. "No worries, man, I'm glad to help. Your little girl is a cutie by the way."

I groan, but can't help the smile that follows. "Thanks. I think I'm going to be in big trouble with her." I slide into the booth and take a long sip of my drink.

The whiskey has a slight burn as it trails down my throat, but it's smooth and just what I need. Jax picks up her spoon and takes a bite of the strawberry cheesecake. I watch as she places the spoon in her mouth, her eyes closing as she moans and slowly pulls the utensil from between her luscious lips. *Fuck. Me. She's making me harder than I've ever been with just a moan and a damn spoon.* As nonchalantly as I can, I re-adjust my growing hard-on.

I down my whiskey, knowing Adam will kill me for taking the good stuff as a shot. No chance in hell am I savoring the flavor with the gorgeous woman next to me practically sucking the spoon off like she would my cock. My throat is dry, and suddenly I need another drink. *Right. Now.*

I clear my throat and lift my glass toward Adam at the bar before placing it on the table and resting my hands around the glass. "So I wanted to see if you might be able to help me figure out the best way to make sure Ella doesn't close in on herself. And to make sure I don't screw things up with her," I explain, focusing my attention on Jax's eyes and not her mouth.

Setting her spoon down, she turns slightly to face me. "I guess the only way I can answer that is to know what your relationship with your daughter is like, or what it was like before her mother passed."

Sighing, I release a breath. *This is going to be a fucking shitty conversation.* "I don't really have a relationship with Ella, or at least not a previous one. I didn't know I had a daughter until last week."

"But that one chick seems like she's known Ella longer than a week. The one that was having the hissy fit when we arrived?" Jax breaks in.

Another glass of amber liquid is placed in front of me. "Thanks, man."

"It's not a shot damn it! This is the good shit. The Yellow Spot." Adam grunts at me but is all smiles for Jax and CJ. "Would either of you like another drink?"

Jax and her friend both order another round, and Adam steps away.

"The drama queen is my younger sister. She's about seven years younger than Nessa and myself. She was Hallie's, Ella's mother, best friend. Seven years ago, Hallie and I had a one night stand, and I knocked her up. She, however, didn't see fit to inform me I had a child," I share. *God, this is way too much info, and with this baggage, I'm not going to be able to get to know Jax as well as I'd like to.*

"What the fuck?" CJ says refocusing on me, and what I just divulged.

"And oh yeah, my sister knew about my daughter but didn't inform the rest of us. Hallie was diagnosed with an aggressive form of ovarian cancer and, instead of terminating Ella, she decided to keep her."

"Holy shit," Jax mutters. She reaches for her glass, which is empty, so she picks up her spoon and takes a bite of the brownie. This time, instead of sucking on the spoon, she flips the utensil over, licking the extra chocolate and whipped cream from it. "Ella's not acting as if she's uncertain about you, though."

More drinks are dropped off, including another for me, and I glance over at Adam. He's shaking his head and Nessa's standing next to him, her mouth slightly open in a half-shocked, half-laughing expression.

Leave it to my twin. Of course she's going to notice how many drinks I have and what torture the woman next to me is putting me through. I take another drink of my whiskey as they leave the booth.

"Needless to say, I'm still getting used to having a child. Ella was told all about me from Piper as she was growing up. So, I'm guessing that's why she's comfortable being around me. The day Hallie finally told me about Ella was the same day she was in the accident that ultimately ended her life. On Tuesday when we stopped into Voodoo, Ella and I had only known each other for a week." I blow out a long, deep breath. *God it feels so fucking good to get that off my chest.*

"Wow. Okay so…. Shit." Jax bites her bottom lip, and all I can think about is doing that myself. *Dude get it together! She's here to talk about Ella and help you with her. Sex can't be in the equation.*

"Yeah well, at least I know about my little girl now, and she's in my life. I just need to make sure she's okay, and that we make this transition with her as easy as possible. I don't want her to think because of the bullshit her mom did that we can't talk about Hallie, or whatever she needs to do to remember her." I drink more of my whiskey, sipping it as I should this time.

Jax looks as if she's really thinking over everything I've just spewed out before she says anything. She's taking her time eating bites of each dessert. Swallowing her last bite, she begins.

"I get that. Mind you, I was in my teens when my mom passed. Not to mention my dad had been in my life from the beginning. But I'm willing to help in whatever way I can. Ella's a sweetheart, and considering everything she's going through, she's pretty open to people in general. Well... maybe not Piper, considering what she said earlier. But there could be other issues going on."

"Don't forget Ella wants to come to the shop tomorrow and have you teach them how to make doughnuts," CJ pipes in.

I chuckle. "She's in love with y'all's donuts. Donuts were her and her mom's thing, so I want to try and keep that going for her, even if we change it into making them ourselves so it blends Hallie into something we do that's ours."

"That will help. Belladonna's open on Sundays right?" Jax asks.

"For brunch, yes. But she and I can come over first thing in the morning, or after my shift. Whichever works best for you. If you're not going to be there, that's fine, too. We can try a different day." I run a hand though my hair as I backtrack.

"Tomorrow's fine. I'll be in most of the day." Jax fidgets, and her leg bumps mine.

"Hey Forest? Wes is asking for you," Adam calls from the bar.

I glance up to acknowledge him, and realize the bar is slowly emptying.

"I guess I should let y'all finish your meal. Thanks for coming in so we could talk. I'll see you tomorrow." I hold out my hand first to Jax then to CJ before sliding out of the booth.

I get about ten steps away when I hear, "Damn girl! Were you trying to flirt with him? If not, you failed. It's a damn good thing you're like my sister, otherwise you'd be up shit creek without a paddle."

"CJ! I wasn't!" There's a pause then I hear Jax say, "I'm drawn to him. And his little girl." It's the last thing I hear from their table.

Shit... maybe I do have a shot with her, even with all the craziness of my life. Bonus: she likes my daughter.

I stroll into the kitchen and, abruptly, cat-calls fill the room. *Motherfucker. What the hell have these shitheads been discussing?*

98

CHAPTER 13

Forest

The alarm blares way too early for a Sunday. However, I can't hit snooze and sleep a little longer. Ella and I have an important date today. Stretching, my back cracks as I try to realign everything after sleeping on the couch again. *I need to pick up an air mattress and talk to the office about renting a bigger place for the two of us. Or maybe I should see what Calla's building has available? At least then I'd have someone closer to help. And a doorman. What the fuck am I thinking? Calla has the same schedule I do.*

I roll my eyes at myself. Time to shower then wake Ella. Tossing the blankets off, I sit up and arch my back a bit more then rub the sleep from my eyes. With a yawn, I push off the couch and head into my shower. Once in the shower, I clean off quickly then just stand under the hot water, letting it melt the tension in my shoulders away.

A knock has me shutting off the spray.

"Daddy?" Ella's voice carries through the door.

"Give me a sec baby girl!" I grab for a towel and dry off quickly before wrapping it around my waist and stepping out of the shower.

I open the bathroom door to find Ella standing there with tears streaming down her face, and my heart aches.

"What's wrong Sweetheart?" I kneel down to her level and pull her into my arms.

"I had a bad dream. I called for you, but you didn't answer, and I got scared," she sobs.

"I'm sorry. I didn't mean to scare you. I'm right here though, and I'm not going anywhere. Okay?" I pick her up and carry her over to the bed. "How about you tell me about this bad dream?"

She nods and wipes her eyes and nose with her nightgown before taking a deep breath then cuddles into my chest.

With a sniffle, Ella begins. "We were at Mom's grave, and I was in the coffin with her, but I was still alive. No one could hear me screaming to get out. You just left... forgetting all about me."

Holy fuck! The beating of my heart speeds up, and it feels like it is going to break through my chest wall.

I tighten my arms around her. "Ella, Sweetheart... now that I know about you, and know that you're mine, I could never forget about you or leave you. At least I couldn't leave you for very long. And if I ever have to do anything where I have to go on a trip without you, I'll make sure you are surrounded with people that love you," I murmur into her hair as my cheek rests on top of her head.

Her arms squeeze me as best she can, and she sniffles again. Warm tears soak into my chest.

"Daddy, do you think with Jax's help I won't be so scared?" she whispers as she pulls back.

"Have you been scared baby girl? You've had such a brave face on since your mom's accident, I didn't realize you were scared. I should have, and I'm so sorry for not seeing that. I'll try to be better at knowing what you need, but I need a little help from you. Okay? Since we're still trying to learn this new way of life, will you try to talk to me when you're feeling scared? Then we can work together to slay whatever is scaring you." I gently wipe the tears from her face.

Ella's lips tremble. "I'll try Daddy. You and Jax already help. I do feel safe when I'm near both of you. Aunt Calla & Aunt Nessa too. I don't feel as safe as I used to around Aunt Piper, though. Last night when she was being a brat, I really didn't want to be near her."

"Well that could be because she *was* acting like a brat, but if it keeps happening we'll see what we can do. Aunt Piper has helped take care of you for a long time, and it's probably hard for her to share you now."

"Daddy, how do you know so much?" The alarm I had set to wake her buzzes, and she slides off my lap.

"Nonna and Gramps, actually. They work with troubled kiddos, so when I was young they would use some of the techniques on me and your aunts when we couldn't explain what was bothering us," I explain, getting to my feet in search of my phone.

Ella follows me into the bathroom where my phone is lying on the counter. As I turn off the alarm, she grabs her toothbrush and turns on the water.

"While you brush your teeth and hair, I'm going to get dressed for work. When you finish, meet me in the kitchen for some breakfast." Placing a hand on her head, I bend to kiss her hair.

"Okay Daddy. Can I wear shorts today?" She sticks her toothbrush in her mouth.

"Yes, you can. You'll have to be careful if you come into the kitchen with shorts on, though." I head out of the bathroom and into the closet.

I quickly dress in my chef pants and a t-shirt before heading to the kitchen. *I need coffee, and I need it now!* On the way to the kitchen, I duck back into the bathroom to grab my phone, and I shoot off a text.

Me: Mom, Ella had a bad nightmare. Can you or Dad talk to her, or tell me who she might need to see?

Mom: Let Dad and I talk to her tomorrow after we pick her up from school. Speaking of, did you add us to the list to pick her up?

Me: Fuck! That was what I forgot to do when I requested her school work. I'll get you added in the morning.

Mom: Make sure you do. Your dad or I will pick her up on Tuesday, too.

Me: Thanks Mom.

Mom: You're welcome. Now, I need to fix breakfast. Enjoy your Sunday. Bye.

Me: Bye.

Needing my coffee fix, I place my phone on the counter and reach for the remaining coffee I ground yesterday. The French press is next to the sink and clean, thankfully, which allows me to quickly start brewing the coffee. As my morning joe steeps, I cook some eggs and bacon for Ella and myself.

"Ella, breakfast is almost ready," I call over my shoulder as I flip bacon.

"Daddy, can I wear this today?" Ella stands between the kitchen and the living room in a yellow dress and a pair of boots.

Smiling, I nod. "You look beautiful. Aunt Nessa is going to love the look."

"Really? Aunt Nessa has some awesome funky clothes. I *really* like them. Mom and Aunt Piper weren't always happy with my choices when it came to clothes."

"Knowing your Aunt Piper, I'm not surprised. Don't get me wrong. Both of your aunts have their own style. They both look good and can control a room with their presence if they choose to. Trust me when I say, now that Aunt Nessa knows about you, she will take you shopping and spoil you.

Just be sure Aunt Calla goes with you guys. She'll keep Aunt Nessa grounded when it comes to what you want to wear."

"Thanks, Daddy. What will Nonna do when she takes me shopping?" She pulls out a bar stool and climbs up.

Chuckling, I plate her eggs and bacon before placing the the breakfast in front of her. "Nonna will make sure you have practical clothes and, most likely, things you can play in and get dirty. If you want to be more rough and tumble, Nonna's the one to shop with. Aunt Calla has a bit of Nonna in her, which is probably why I love working with her so much." I hand over a fork, and Ella takes a bite of her eggs.

She swallows her bite. "Daddy, have you *ever* dated Aunt Calla?" Ella questions, picking up a slice of bacon.

"No. Until a year ago she was engaged, and Uncle Wes is in love with her, even though he won't tell her. Calla is one of my best friends. You know how Jax had her guy friend with her last night?" Ella nods. "Well, that's Calla for me. She's like... one of the guys. I can talk to her about anything, even girly stuff I don't want to talk to Aunt Nessa about." I lean in toward Ella as I dramatically whisper the last part.

Her bottom lip sticks out slightly in a small pout. "That's how I felt with my friends from the team back home. I haven't found the same since moving here."

"You've just started school here. Let's give it a month or two before you decide to hate it. Granted, we need a new place that has enough room for everything. You feel like house hunting tomorrow after school?"

She scrunches her nose. "Ugh. Do we have to?"

"How about this... while you finish your homework at Belladonna today, write down a list of all the things you want in a place to live, and when we head over to Voodoo Doughnut to see Jax, we'll discuss it? Does that sound better?" I take a sip of my coffee before taking my first bite of eggs and bacon.

Before answering, Ella finishes the food on her plate and hops off the stool to put the plate and fork in the sink. She walks over to sit next to me.

"I can manage that. I didn't like house hunting with Mom, but she didn't ask me what I wanted. I wanted us to be close to you, and she picked the rental house across town," she grumbles, placing her arms on the counter before resting her head on them.

I smoothe her hair back and finish my breakfast so we can make it to Belladonna on time.

CHAPTER 14

Forest

As soon as Ella and I walk into Belladonna, Nessa is glued to Ella's side telling her how cute her outfit is, just like I said she would, and pulling her toward the bar. I'm barely able to kiss her head before Nessa has Ella out of my sight. I chuckle as I make my way into the kitchen.

"Damnit! Motherfucker! Why the hell won't this work?" I hear Calla yell as I step through the doors.

Glancing around, I find the kitchen empty except for Calla standing at one of the stoves. The clatter of a pan tells me she's pissed at whatever she was trying to make. She growls, and I force myself not to laugh. The woman is so fiery it's cute.

"Breathe woman," I tell her, and she jumps. "Sorry. What were you trying to make?" I step further into the kitchen.

"I wanted to make something special for Ella today. I know she likes grilled cheese sandwiches, but I wanted to make her something a little more. And I fucking can't do it. Fucking asshole still controls me! Why the fuck can't I get him out of my system?" Her hands ball into fists, and I know if we had something for her to beat, like a punching bag, she'd be using it right about now.

Maybe we should think about getting one of those for the office?

I move into her personal space and wrap my arms around her. "Right now, I think Ella's going to be happy with anything you fix her. Hell, she'd be happy with you taking her down to see Jax, but Sweetheart, we have *got* to get Torrance out of your head." She glares at me. "I know you want him out of there," I kiss the top of her head, "but he's not gone yet. It doesn't help that he's also a food critic and keeps giving you shitty reviews when he doesn't even step one foot in our door."

"I know. And I *know* I need to exorcise him. I might need a road trip to New Orleans to see a Voodoo Priestess," she quips, glancing back at the pan.

"Maybe instead of going down to New Orleans you could go see Jax and have her make you a Voodoo Doll of Torrance. It would be cheaper." I smirk down at her. She sucker punches me in the gut, and we both crack up laughing.

"I think I'm going to steal Ella and do just that. But first, I was thinking of making Ella mac and cheese with a sandwich. Do you think she'd eat it? At the rate that was going," she gestures to the pan with something burnt inside of it, "I'm going to need a little help." Calla gives me a side hug.

"Hell, I'm not sure. I really suck at this parenting thing," I reply, raking my hand through my hair.

"No, you don't. She's only been in the family for a little over a week. We're all dealing with a learning curve here. I'll go ask her what she'd like with the mac and cheese." Raising up on her tiptoes, Calla kisses my cheek before backing away from me and grabbing the pot once again.

I move to my station, stopping to plug my phone into the speakers. I select one of the playlists and push play. *House Party* by Sam Hunt fills the room, and before long, everything becomes background noise as I mix my batters and bake the bread. It's not until Calla and Ella enter the kitchen some time later that I realize I've zoned out for the last hour or so.

"Daddy! Aunt Calla took me down to see Jax. I was good and didn't even get any donuts since I know we're going back down there after work. Aunt Calla got two Voodoo Dolls, and we're going to stab them a few times. She also said she wants me to help make mac and cheese, if it's okay with you? Can I please? Mac and cheese is my favorite!" Ella announces in a rush. I swear she doesn't even take a breath when she says all of that.

"Hey! No fair! Mac and cheese is my speciality. You're not allowed to steal it." Wes rushes up to Ella, picking her up and tickling her until she's laughing hard. "I think each of us should make a batch and let you taste them. Kind of like a little cook-off. Then you can decide who makes the best. We've been having this disagreement for years. What do you think, Munchkin?" Wes proposes. The glee that radiates off Ella is infectious, and I can't help but grin.

"Now you've done it. This kitchen is going to be at war for the rest of the day." I laugh as she rubs her tiny hands together. If I didn't know any better, I'd think this was all a part of her evil plot.

Trey calls out an order and steps over to our little group, smirking.

"So Ella, what do you think? Should we add mac and cheese as a special today for brunch? Maybe add a BLT with it?" Trey messes with her hair as he questions her.

"Can we?" She's so excited she's squirming in Wes's arms.

"Let's ask Calla. You want to drag her in here?" Wes carefully puts Ella back on her feet.

"I'm right here," Calla calls as she waltzes into the kitchen with a box of donuts. "What's going on? Ella and I need to put a few more holes in this donut and make some mac and cheese." Calla sets the donuts on her normal station.

"Aunt Calla, can we do a mac and cheese…. What did you call it Uncle Wes?" She turns slightly to look up at him.

"A mac and cheese cook-off." A shit-eating grin forms on Wes's face.

Damn, this is going to get ugly.

"Yeah that! And Uncle Trey says we can make the mac

and cheese as a special today for brunch. If it's okay with you?" my baby girl answers, her big doe eyes pleading with Calla to do this for her.

"You two fucking suck. You are total assholes for using Ella like this." Calla points at Wes and Trey then kneels down to Ella's level. "I think we might need to start a swear jar for you. To answer your question and request, yes, we can do a cook-off and use the different mac and cheeses as specials today. Aaaaand... I think you should name them." Calla smiles at Ella as she jumps up and down.

Calla's not wrong. I think we're going to need a few swear jars. At least two here, one at our place, and probably one at Mom and Dad's. I should probably pick them up today after we finish at Voodoo Doughnut. Hell, at the rate we're going, we'll all be paying for her college education!

I notice the glare Calla gives Wes and Trey when Ella isn't looking. Calla gets to her feet, and the kitchen staff gets back to work as Calla, Wes, and Trey make their way to their stations. I cross my fingers and pray that Calla can pull this off today. Maybe this is what she needs to kick start her mojo. Hell, I can't remember the last time she's even wanted to try to create something special, yet, having my little girl here is giving her ideas.

"Ella? You going to help me, or do you want to hang with your dad for a bit?" Calla calls over her shoulder.

"I want to help *you!*" Ella replies, excitedly. "Is there something I can stand on so I'm taller?"

"Stay right here and I'll find the stool Aunt Calla needs

when she's in the walk-in." I move to look for the stepstool as three of my best friends start trash-talking each other. "But after you're done helping, you need to get more homework finished. Okay?" I remind Ella.

"You going to make your boring old noodles with no flavor?" Trey baits Wes as he glances over at the ingredients laying out on Wes's station.

"No flavor? At least Ella will be able to swallow mine! Yours is always so dry," Wes counters, laughing.

Shaking my head, I find the stool and carry it over to Calla's station. Ella follows, stepping up to the counter as soon as I have the stool in place.

"Daddy, why are they being mean to each other?" she wonders, furrowing her brows.

Calla leans down and whispers, "They're trying to screw with each other's head." Then her voice raises. "They're acting like little boys." She winks at Ella, and I head back to my side of the kitchen where it's safe.

The taunting goes on for a while longer. Trey and Wes even add Calla into their harassment, which shocks the hell out of me considering her lack of confidence in the kitchen as of late. Yet, the playfulness is refreshing, and I've missed it. As the taunts, jabs, and trash-talk proceed, the atmosphere in the kitchen changes. It's as if a weight is finally beginning to lift from the room.

Timers sound off, and Ella hops off her step stool. Calla hands her three different spoons, as she has throughout this contest, so Ella could taste the three different roux. Now, each mac and cheese is plated differently, and all three are making my mouth water.

"Alright young lady! Time for you to choose," Wes tells her.

Ella moves around the kitchen to each station, taking small bites of each dish. *It's like she's a fucking pro at this.* She frowns, and her bottom lip juts out slightly. Placing the last spoon on the counter, her hands go to her hips, and she huffs. Holy hell it's cute, but I know in a few years I'm going to hate that pose.

"I can't decide. I really like all three. Can I have a bowl with them all mixed together?" she requests, and everyone laughs. "What? I really wanted to pick a winner, but I just *can't!*"

"Darlin' we know. And you did great. Have you decided what we should call the special today?" Trey steps up to her, holding out his hand for Ella to high-five him.

"How about... Ella's Mac and Cheese!" she pronounces, giggling.

"Done!" Calla shouts, triumphantly. "Now let's get you a bowl, and one of Trey's amazing BLT's so you can finish that homework for Dad."

Ella runs over to me, and I squat down to put myself on her level. "Thanks for letting me be here today, Daddy. I love coming to work with you." She kisses my cheek and heads out of the kitchen, Calla following behind her with the bowl of mac and cheese and the sandwich.

"Dude. I think I speak for all of us when I say, I love that little girl," Wes announces from across the kitchen.

"Agreed," Trey adds.

Damn. She is one special little girl, and fuck if she's not going to have all of us wrapped around her little finger.

CHAPTER 15

Ella

Finishing my three mac and cheese brunch, and Trey's yummy BLT, I pull out my homework for the week. Now I understand why Mom hated it so much when I missed school. Trying to catch up is for the birds. But I don't think I could've handled being at school last week. Spending the time with Daddy and learning some of the ins and outs of Belladonna kept me from being so sad about Mom too much. I haven't told Daddy yet, but I'm not sure I want to go to Mom's grave ever again. Especially not after having that dream this morning.

"Hey kiddo! I've got you something," Uncle Adam announces as he steps up to the booth where I'm sitting in the bar area.

Everyone keeps sitting me at this table as it's the easiest one to watch me. He eyes my books and papers spread all over the table.

"You have a shit-ton of homework." He pushes a book over as he sits next to me on the bench seat.

"Yep. Oh, and Aunt Calla said she's going to get a swear jar for y'all for cussing in front of me. I didn't have the nerve to tell her I've heard worse at the football games with Mom."

Uncle Adam laughs. "Well, she has a point. We *should* watch our language in front of you. With that said, Uncle Wes alone will put enough money in the jar for you to go to college before you hit high school." He winks.

"You think so? Okay, maybe I like this idea!" I grin. *Not that I really want to take Uncle Wes's money.*

"That's my girl." Uncle Adam ruffles my hair.

I smack at his hand. "So what is this present you got for me?" I ask as one of the waitresses refills my cup with water. "Thank you," I tell her, and my attention goes back to Uncle Adam.

"This," he places a wrapped present in front of me. "I know it gets loud in here, and I can't imagine it's easy to do your homework with all the racket. Don't let your Aunt Piper know, though. She'll get even more pissed if her attitude about you being here is any indication."

I giggle. He's not lying. Aunt Piper is being a royal pain in the butt about me being at the restaurant so much. What she doesn't realize is that it's the best way for me to get to know my new family. Or maybe she does realize it, and she just isn't happy I'm not living with her anymore. After the conversations I've heard since she's been here, I'm surprised she even told me about Daddy as I was growing up. I'm not the least bit shocked she didn't tell the family about me, or push Mom to tell them. I think she would've been happy if they'd never known about me.

Ripping into the wrapping paper, I find a new phone. My face scrunches up. "Uncle Adam, I don't think anyone's going to be happy with me having this." I hold the box out toward him.

"Actually, we all will. However, we *will* monitor what goes on the damn thing. I talked to Forest about it before I ordered it." He grins, and it makes his eye sparkle as if he's doing something he shouldn't. "We'll program everyone's number in it then add some music so you can put the earbuds in and ignore all of us when you're here doing your homework. Tonight, have Forest order a case and earbuds that you like. You may want to talk to Aunt Calla before he orders them, though. She has small ears and wears earbuds all the time when she runs so she can tell your dad the best ones to get for you."

I lean in and give him a huge hug. He hugs me back before kissing my head and scooting out of the booth, getting back to work.

I can't wait to set the new phone up. I'd had one before, but I don't know what happened to it. It's been missing since we moved here. Sticking the phone in my backpack, I pull the book Uncle Adam had moved back into place and try to get back to work. That is, until I hear Aunt Piper's voice.

Really??? Not today! I was hoping I'd get to have a break from her.

"Ben, are you sure we should be meeting here?" I hear her ask someone.

Ben? Is this the same Ben she's been talking to for months? He's here?

"Piper, I haven't seen my sister all that much between Hallie's passing, and her running this place. So yes, I wanted to come here. Why don't you want any of your family to know we talk?" Ben replies. His voice is deep, and I know I've heard it before.

Even though I don't want the griping Aunt Piper is going to give me, I want to see what Ben looks like. Sliding out of the booth, I see Aunt Nessa heading this direction. She makes a gesture for me to get back to the table.

"Ben, it's nice to see you again. Should I let Calla know you're here?" Aunt Nessa asks.

"Yes, please, Nessa. How are you?"

"Good, actually. Piper, how about you don't make a scene today while you're here?" There's a pause. Then Aunt Nessa tells them, "Why don't you look over the menu while I let Calla know you're here? Your server will be with you shortly. And in case you want something that's not on the menu, you should ask about today's mac and cheese special."

"Why would we want mac and cheese?" Aunt Piper demands with the attitude I've heard many times.

"Because Ella helped get Calla in a cooking mood. She even helped Calla, Wes, and Trey as they each created a special mac and cheese dish for her today," Aunt Nessa says smuggly. I lean over, peering under the table to see her wink at me before walking off.

I have a strange family.

Jax

TODAY HAS GONE by so fucking slowly, even though we've been swamped since churches let out. I keep staring at the clock to see if Belladonna is closed yet. When Calla and Ella came in this morning, my excitement was through the roof. I love seeing that little girl, and her dad isn't too shabby to look at either. I can't remember the last time I was tied in knots over a guy, and I've never wanted to spend time with a kid until Ella. Every time I see her, I can't believe her mom just passed. I was a wreck for months after my mom died. And while I see the shadows under her eyes from her grief, she's doing fucking awesome for her age.

"Stop pacing. You're going to wear out the floor," CJ mutters as he walks in the kitchen. "You know, I've never seen you this twitchy. You really like him don't you?"

"Yes," I sigh. "I barely know the man, but anytime I know I might see him I get butterflies in my belly, and my heart races. I'm fucked if he's not interested in me in any other way except to help Ella." I glance down at my watch then back at the batch of dough in front of me.

"You're going to break poor Bradley's heart, you know," CJ chuckles, coming to stand next to me and patting my shoulder.

I grin. "As if you care. Besides, he's like my baby brother," I remind him, picking up the roller.

"Yeah, well... my brother's a little thick when it comes to you." He shakes his head and leans against the counter. "You sure you're ready for this? I know I've asked before, but helping with Ella might be harder than you think, considering your past."

I think about it for a minute as I roll out the dough. "I have to face my demons at some point. Maybe if I can help Ella, I'll be able to help myself, too."

"That's a healthy way to look at it. I hope it works. They seem nice, so I'd hate to have to kick Forest's ass."

I bust out laughing. CJ waves me off, rolling his eyes at me as he walks away. Focusing on the task at hand, I begin cutting the Cock-N-Balls so they'll be finished by the time Forest and Ella come in. Earlier, Ella seemed really interested in making the Voodoo Dolls since Calla wanted two of them.

"Jax, there's someone here that wants to talk to you," a female voice calls back. *I need to figure out the new girls' voices. They sound so similar.*

I look up to see who else is in the kitchen. There are a few of our staff back here. "Can one of y'all finish these for me?"

"Sure thing, Jax," one of the staff replies as I leave the kitchen.

As soon as I step into the main room, Ella is waving at me from the other side of the glass cases. She's so fucking cute it's not even funny. I point to an open table for Forest and Ella to sit at then I pull three different doughnuts from the case. Before I can step out from behind the displays, CJ comes back out.

"I'll bring over some drinks. After you talk with them are you leaving for the day?" He's grabbing three cups from their spot by the register as he asks the question.

"Thanks. Yeah, probably. I want to try and chill for the rest of the afternoon. Maybe finish the book I started the other night. Oh hey! Remember I won't be here tomorrow," I say over my shoulder.

"You need a break. Now that we've hired the new people, we'll both be able to have a few more days off." He smiles and shoos me off as he starts on the drinks.

I have to stop once as one of the other young patrons runs in front of me, and I almost drop the doughnuts I'm carrying.

"Sorry," the female following the little boy says. "I don't think I should've let him have the whole doughnut. His mom's going to kill me for this sugar high." She chuckles as she passes me.

I snort. Not sure what she expected, bringing the boy to a doughnut shop, but whatever. I don't have to watch the kid.

CHAPTER 16

Forest

Icringe when the little boy runs right in front of Jax. Honestly, I'm not sure how she stopped in time. I thought for sure she was going to fall on top of the kid. My attention falls back on Ella. Her jaw has dropped, and if mom was here, she'd tell her to close her mouth so flies don't get in.

"Young lady," I begin, making sure I have her full attention. "Please never do that in a restaurant. Not only could you hurt yourself, but you could also hurt the person carrying the food. Not to mention then the kitchen staff has to fix everything, and the customers get pissy when they don't get their meal in a timely fashion." She nods.

"Don't worry, Daddy. I won't. Besides, I think Aunt Nessa would make me clean up the mess if I did." Her body is almost vibrating with nervous energy.

What is going on in that head of hers to make her this fidgety? "You're probably right on that," I agree. "So... you said you finished your homework, finally, but you didn't tell me if you got the list for what you'd like for us to have in our new place finished."

Before Ella can answer me, Jax is at the table placing the donuts down and taking a seat next to Ella. My little girl beams at Jax.

"Drinks will be right out. CJ is bringing them over." Jax glances between Ella and me then rips off a piece of the apple fritter she brought over. "So, how was your day Ella?"

Holy shit! This woman just asked my daughter how her day was before asking me.

That one simple question settles Ella. She looks up at me then back at the donut with sprinkles. Yep, she's definitely my daughter when it comes to sweets. I always went for the sprinkles when I was a kid, too. I bump her with my elbow, and she glances back up at me. I nod, and she picks up the donut and takes a huge bite. I can't hold back my laugh. The bite is way too big for her little mouth, and I'm praying she doesn't choke on it.

"I see I picked the right doughnut for Ella. What about you?" Jax wants to know as she tears another piece from the fritter.

"Is it cream filled?" I ask as CJ walks up to the table.

His right eyebrow raises as he places the drinks on the table then he moves each drink in front of us. *How the hell does he know what Ella and I drink? I don't think Jax could guess that one.*

"Really? Cream filled in front of this little beauty?" he jokes, smirking.

I bust out laughing again.

"CJ! He was asking about the doughnut." Jax chuckles. "What did you bring this Sweetheart to drink?" she inquires, touching Ella's silky hair to move it out of her face.

"What you used to drink with doughnuts... chocolate milk. You get a chai today, and Forest has coffee. It's black. I wasn't sure what you take in it."

"Oh I think she's going to love you even more than she already does, Jax, for the chocolate milk. Thankfully she's already finished her homework, otherwise I might be in trouble with all this sugar going in her." I grin as Ella scrunches up her face at me. "Black is great," I tell CJ. "Thanks, man." I pick up the cup and nod before taking a sip.

CJ eyes Jax for a minute then walks off.

"He's protective," I observe as Jax takes a sip of her own drink.

"He is. He's like the brother I never had. Anyway... you guys wanted to discuss maybe making doughnuts as a way to connect, or helpful ideas to get Ella through the tough times?"

Does that mean she doesn't want to help? Shit... and I was hoping to ask her out on a date, too. One day.

"Learning to make donuts would be cool. Maybe we could do a cook-off like we did with the mac and cheese at Belladonna. That was fun," Ella pipes in, shifting in her seat to look between Jax and me then taking another bite of the donut.

"A mac and cheese cook-off?" Jax questions, finishing her apple fritter.

I shake my head, smiling at my daughter before answering Jax. "Yes. It seems that, after leaving you this morning, Calla and Ella decided they wanted mac and cheese. So when they returned to Belladonna, that's what Calla was fixing. Needless to say, both Trey and Wes wanted in on this action, so they decided to have a cook-off, and Ella was the judge." I take my first bite of the cream-filled donut Jax picked for me.

A grin forms on Jax's face, and she covers her mouth with her hand. She has a beautiful smile, and her eyes light up whenever one crosses those luscious lips of hers. Her pale green eyes also sparkle when she looks at Ella. A jab to my side has me blinking and pulling my attention from Jax to Ella.

"Yes baby girl?" I ask, rubbing my side.

"Are you okay Daddy?" Ella's voice is soft, and there's a quiver in it that hasn't been there all day.

"I'm okay. Did you say something, and I didn't answer?" There are tears filling her eyes, and I pull her into my lap before wiping the two that sit at the corners away.

"You went still and weren't talking. It worried me." She's holding on to me as tightly as she can.

"I'm so sorry Sweetheart. I didn't mean to scare you. I'll let you in on a secret... I was mesmerized by Jax's green eyes. They're like your baby blue ones. Sometimes I just can't stop staring into them, and I get lost."

"She does have pretty eyes," Ella agrees. "Do you really think mine are as pretty as hers?" She lifts her head up so we're making eye contact.

"I do." I kiss her nose. "How about we finish this snack, and maybe Jax will sit with us as we talk about a new place to live?" I peer over at Jax, and she nods.

Ella scoots off my lap and sits back in her chair. She picks up a napkin and wipes her face one more time before eating a little more of her donut and drinking her milk.

"You're thinking of moving?" Jax inquires, but Ella puts her hand up in a stopping gesture.

"Can we please talk about the donut cook-off?" Ella whines shoving her hands together in a praying motion.

Jax and I both laugh. *I really fucking love this kid.*

"If you and your dad find someone else that can bake, I will gladly have a doughnut cook-off with you." Jax smiles down at Ella.

"Really?! Yessss!" Ella drags out the 's' and pumps her fist next to her face.

Once again she has me shaking my head. My phone

buzzes with an incoming text, and I pull it out of my back pocket.

Wes: I know you're down at Voodoo, but we're thinking about heading out to Brewtorium in a bit and wanted to see if you want to join?

Me: Sure, Ella and I can make it. We can't hang out long since she has to be at school early tomorrow morning.

Wes: That's cool. My brothers and Ben just informed Calla and I that they head out tomorrow. They have to get back to camp.

Me: Well damn. I guess Piper will be heading down to Houston, as well. I'll make sure we're there. I'd like to say bye to everyone, and I'm sure Ella will want to see Piper if she's there.

Wes: Good deal. I think we'll head over about 4.

Me: See you there.

"Everything okay?" Jax asks as she turns her attention on me.

"Yes. Wes was letting me know everyone's getting together later to send off his brothers and Calla's tonight." I set my phone on the table.

"Daddy, is Aunt Calla's brother Aunt Piper's boyfriend?" Ella glances up at me.

I do a double take, not sure what would make Ella ask that question. "I don't know, Sweetheart. Why do you ask?"

"They were at Belladonna together today. I've heard his voice before, but I can't remember from where," she answers then pulls her backpack off the floor and opens it. She takes out the box with the phone Adam said he was getting for her, along with a spiral notebook and pencil.

"Whatcha doing Ella?" I grab her bag and place it back on the ground for her.

"Writing down things I want our new place to have. And Uncle Adam said we need to get me a cover for the new phone and earbuds. But he said I should talk to Aunt Calla about those." She flips open the notebook and her little tongue sticks out slightly.

"New place?" Jax's expression is perplexed. "Why do y'all need a new place?"

"Daddy doesn't have room for all of his stuff *and* mine. Plus, he's sleeping on the couch so I can have his bed," Ella tells her quickly and starts writing ideas down.

"I want Ella to have her own room and, while I do have a two bedroom apartment, it would be really nice if we could have a three bedroom place. I want her input, so I told her to write down everything she wants. That way I can try to find what makes us both happy." I lean toward Ella and kiss her head.

"What about where she and her mom were living?" Jax poses.

"I don't want to stay there," Ella replies, her lips trembling. "I didn't like it before the accident, and I really don't want to be there now."

"The only thing we need to go back there for is to clean it out. I'll see if the guys will help me with that tomorrow, so you don't have to go back. Okay?" I offer, wrapping my arms around her.

"Thanks, Daddy."

The three of us discuss features Ella would like our new place to include, and possibly adding a pet to the house. For the most part, Jax doesn't add much to the conversation. Her presence is calming, though, which is helpful. We get the list completed fairly quickly, and Jax gives us some pointers on ways to make the transition between my place to the new place easier, as well as advice about adding Hallie and Ella's stuff from their old place. Ella gets teary as we discuss Hallie, and says, a few times, that she doesn't want any of her Mom's things in the new place. Jax gently reminds her it will help as the days go by, and Hallie's not here.

Ella even fills Jax in about her dream this morning. Before Ella finishes the story, Jax has her in her lap, and she's rocking her. If the moment hadn't been so emotional for all of us, I would've taken a picture of the two of them. The sight of them together fills my heart, even though I haven't had either of them in my life for very long. *And really, I can't even claim to have Jax.*

"Jax, will you go out with us tonight?" Ella pipes up as we gather our belongings.

"Oh Sweetie, I'm not sure that would be appropriate since it's just family," Jax remarks, kneeling down to hug Ella.

"Please?" Ella begs, hugging Jax tighter.

"Join us," I encourage, reaching my hand out to help Jax to her feet. "No one will mind. Then we can talk about another cook-off and dinner tomorrow night."

Jax smiles mischievously. "How can I say no to discussions of a doughnut cook-off? Fair warning, there will be trash talk. I promise you. As for dinner, let's see how tonight goes with your friends. Then maybe we can make plans for tomorrow night."

Damn, I'm screwed! Jax may very well have me wrapped around her finger before the end of the night. What am I going to do with these two precious ladies? Both of them have stolen my heart in only a few short days.

EPILOGUE

Wes

It's been a hell of a long ass two weeks. The only week that seemed longer was when Calla found Torrance with another woman. We didn't get anything cool out of that bullshit like Forest did out of this, though. It's hard to believe, but Forest finding out he has a kid brought some overdue life back into all of us. Now if we can just get back to some kind of normal, things will be good.

Well, having Ella in the family now will be a little different, but I wouldn't want it any other way. Except that Zoe keeps hinting she wants a baby, and I just want to kick her out of the fucking apartment. *Why the fuck did I want her living with me?* At least she's not with us this afternoon. Hell, she'd probably be hanging all over Ben, or one of my brothers if she was.

Someone pats me on my back, and I blink out of my thoughts of Zoe. For the last hour Ben and my brothers have been talking about training camp. I've zoned out, I'm not sure how many times. It's not that football doesn't interest me. It does. Hell, growing up in Texas, how could it not? It's practically a religion down here. Until I got hurt in college, I would have tried to follow in my brothers' footsteps, but blowing out my knee killed that dream. Plus, I wouldn't be working with Calla if that hadn't happened.

"This is a pretty cool place," Ben remarks as he places a new Dubbel Nutz in front of me.

"Yeah. Chris and Whitney have created a fucking awesome hangout. We don't get to come over here that often, but when we do we have a great time," I state before taking a sip of my beer.

I glance around the table. Everyone seems relaxed, and I'm fucking greatful Calla suggested doing this after we closed for brunch.

Ben looks at his sister. "I'm glad you came out tonight. You work too hard, and I worry about you becoming a hermit."

Calla flips Ben off. "I'm allowed to be a hermit if I want."

"Calla, it's been a year. Torrance was an asshole, and I never should've approved of him. I honestly didn't think you two would last as long as you did. I know he was one of our frat brothers, but still... he was a tool, and I didn't realize it until it was too late." Ben frowns.

"None of us realized he was a tool," Sam, my oldest brother, adds.

The rest of us that know Torrance nod in agreement. Hell, if Trey, Rex, or I had known he was a douche back then, we would have stepped in and kicked his ass. Some days I still want to. *Bastard.*

"I worry about you when I can't visit," Ben asserts before he drinks more of his beer.

The shareables we ordered arrive at the table, and they look fucking amazing. I can't decide if I want to try one of the Brat-Stickers, a Pot Sticker, or the Mac and Beer Cheese. Calla always wants the soft pretzel, but she never gets one because it's something she and Ben used to get when their parents were alive. I made sure to order one so she can share it with Ben.

Calla sighs. "I'm not ready to date again, Ben. I'm happy just being one of the boys right now. I don't have to get dolled up or act happy to be out with a guy. I can just... hang." She pulls a piece off the pretzel and pops it in her mouth.

I seriously hate that Calla thinks she's just one of the guys. Yet, that's how we all treat her, because Ben would kick our asses, and my brothers would help, if we treated her any other way.

However, Ben isn't wrong. Calla does need to get out, date, and move on. And if I wasn't such a chicken shit, I would've stepped in before Torrance could hurt her. But I *am* a chicken shit, and I didn't want Ben to kick my ass for touching his sister. He fucking threatened all of our frat brothers during our undergrad years. Now, because of that, Calla and I are stuck in this friend zone, and I'm living with a woman I can't stand.

"I just don't want you to give up because of one asshole," Ben tries again, his expression thoughtful.

Trey bumps my elbow and gives me a stern look. *Yep, Trey knows.* We've been talking about getting Calla out of the kitchen for a night or two. It's not like that would hurt us. Hell, ever since Torrance cheated on her, Calla's cooking has been... lacking. Well, lacking isn't the right word. It's been downright horrific, as if she never learned to cook in the first place. But I have to admit, this morning when we did the mac and cheese cook-off for Ella, Calla fucking kicked ass. I'm glad Ella was the judge because, hands down, I would have picked Calla's dish. It was the first time in almost a year I could taste the magic that is Calla's cooking. *We fucking need that back. Now.*

"How about when you stop serial fucking every piece of ass that walks by, I'll start dating? Deal?" Calla's eyes shift down the table to where Ella is sitting between Forest and Jax. Ella's working on something, or at least pretending to. I can just make out the smirk on her cute little face.

"Damn it! Sorry, Forest. Remind me to pay the jar on Tuesday."

Forest chuckles. "I swear she'll be able to go to any

college she wants before we stop cursing around her." He ruffles Ella's hair.

"What the hell Calla? Do you really think I do that? Pay what jar?" I hear Ben ask but my attention is elsewhere.

"I need another beer. Anyone else?" Calla stands from the bench.

Jax holds up her glass, as does Nessa. With a nod, Calla marches away from the table in a huff. Even when she's in this pissy of a mood, I want to yank her into my arms and kiss the hell out of her. But I can't. Ben would freak the fuck out, especially since he knows some of my more... erotic tendencies. Yeah, making Calla mine isn't in the cards. *But I fucking want her. No other woman turns me the fuck on like Calla. She doesn't even need to be dolled up to do that. She just needs to be herself.*

Ben shifts on the bench so he's facing Trey and me. "Seriously, I need you guys to get her out of this shell," Ben says, glancing around the table and dropping his voice a bit more so no one hears him. "I hate that she's still not herself. I want my baby sister back."

"We all want her back, man. The question is, what can we do that won't make you kill us afterwards?" I mention, staring Ben down. His voice isn't low enough for this discussion to be just between us.

"Wes, I don't care what you have to do, just don't fuck her," Ben replies, taking a long pull of his beer.

My eyes travel down the table as I hear my brother's laugh followed by Trey's, Forest's, and Adam's as Nessa just shakes her head. The only eyes not on us are Ella's, and I'm thankful. *Shit. This is not a conversation I want to be having with Ben while surrounded by all my friends.*

"You just gave Wes free rein to date Calla. You realize that, right?" my jackass middle brother, Noah, says.

Sam slaps the back of his head. "Asshat."

"No, I didn't, because if Wes ever dated my sister, he'd try to fuck her. And I think we can all agree that Wes wants to live." Now Ben's voice does drop, so no one but me can hear him. "We both know she's not a sub, and you like your subs along with your kink."

I swallow hard. He's right. I do like subs and kink, but Calla is different. Even if all we ever had was vanilla sex, I'd take it. *But only for her.* Throat now dry, I pick up my beer and finish the pint.

"I just have to ask... why not let her find herself again?" Jax is curious as she finishes her beer.

It's a good question, and since she's the only one that hasn't known Calla long, I understand why she's asking. And the way she's looking at me then glancing at Ben, I know there's another question she wants to ask but isn't going to. At least not with Ben around.

"Because that tool broke something in Calla, and I'm not here to fix her," Ben replies.

"So pushing her friends to fix her is your answer? Have you asked her how she feels? Does she have confidence in herself anymore? Why don't you tell her how wonderful she is instead of trying to 'fix' her?" Jax uses air quotes when she says the word fix. *Damn. Forest needs to keep this woman.*

Jax is a fucking smart one. She fits into our group like she's always been here. She might even bring the fucker out of his shell, and if Ella gets her way, she'll make sure they keep Jax.

I fucking want what Forest has, and dammit, I want it with Calla! How the fuck am I going to go about getting it? And more importantly... keep Ben from killing me in the process?

NEED MORE SWEET STORIES THAT DONUT CONTAIN CARBS? CHECK OUT:

Donut Be Shy by FG Adams
Love and Donuts by Amy Briggs
Donut Leave Me by Teresa Crumpton
Donut Swipe Right by Tracie Douglas
11 Enticing Donuts by Fifi Flowers
Donut Go Breaking My Heart by Felicia Fox
Donut Hole by Regina Frame
Donuts Dilemma by Jessika Klide
Donut Tease Me by Kristen Luciani
Donut Be Easy by Kristen Hope Mazzola
Donut Tucker Out by Mayra Statham
Donut Overthink It by Shantel Tessier
Five Alarm Donuts by Winter Travers

Find all of the Donut Day Collaboration books here:
http://www.kristenhopemazzola.com/donuts.html

ABOUT THE AUTHOR

Teresa Crumpton is a hybrid: she grew up in the Midwest and the American South. She writes dark supernatural thrillers and contemporary romance. She loves classic horror movies and Shakespeare. She never thought she'd turn her passion for writing into a career, but here she is!

When Teresa isn't writing, you can find her at book signings or traveling the world with the perfect man for her. She's living the dream and keeping a promise she made to her father before he passed.

STAY CONNECTIONED WITH TERESA CRUMPTON:
http://www.teresacrumpton.com

ALSO BY TERESA CRUMPTON

THE FOSTER HOUSE LEGACY SERIES

Her Legacy

Bloodties (Coming Oct. 31, 2018)

ONE OF THE BOYS

Donut Leave Me

Calla's Kitchen

ACKNOWLEDGMENTS

Lucas, love, what can I say? You're my rock. I couldn't do this without you.

Along with my Mom, Charla, I need to thank my dads, Chip and Dennis, and my stepmom, Lynda. You guys have loved and supported me through it all – Love you guys.

My editor gets a big thank you! Steph, love you babe.

Annessa, thanks for keeping me sane. And Allen, thanks for making sure I roll my eyes and smile at least once a day. You don't know how much it actually helps.

Clyde, Chris R, Whitney, and Brewtorium – thanks for... well, you guys know. I hope you enjoy!

Kristen... girl thanks for all the support and everything you do. It's time to go celebrate once again!

Mayra and the rest of the Donut Day Authors - This was a blast ladies! Thanks for letting me join in the fun.

CALLA'S KITCHEN

SNEAK PEEK

CHAPTER 1

CALLA

Austin's brisk morning air is helping to clear my head. I desperately need physical exercise after the nightmare I'd had. Again. Why, after almost a year, I still relived the worst night of my life is beyond me. For what has to have been the hundredth time, this morning's dream replayed the moment I walked in on my friend, lover, and fiancée in bed with another woman. In our bed, of all places! And I just couldn't relive that moment one more time. Not today, of all days.

Today is the anniversary of that humiliating act. So, instead of staying in bed, I'm up before the sun is shining through my bedroom window and heading to the Ann and Roy Butler Trail. It is one of a handful of places that can clear the filth out of my mind.

Unlike my usual short runs, today's run needs to be long

and hard. If I could run the ten-mile trail twice, I would. But only once around will have to do today. I have too many things to do at my restaurant, Belladonna, so I can't spend all day on the trail. The emotional baggage of my past isn't going to make this week any easier, so I really can't be too late getting there.

By the time I reach my destination, the early morning rays of sun are shining over the city and sparkling on Lady Bird Lake. The lake runs south into the Colorado River, where buildings can be seen at its eastern edge. As I start my warm up, the I-35 cream and burnt-red bridge comes into view off in the distance. At six-thirty, the traffic is already starting to build, and I can make out a few semi-trailers, SUVs, and trucks at a dead stop.

With my earbuds in and music blaring, I zone out and allow my legs to take over. The burning starts at mile marker five, but I'm not stopping. I can't quit yet. The visions from my nightmare are still flashing in my mind each time I close my eyes. I have to keep going until I can block them, and the pain, once again. The pain from running is nothing compared to the tension that's knotted every muscle in my body these last few months. Between the food critics' negative reviews, and my ex-fiancée's wedding announcement yesterday, my body desperately needs a good, hard tension reliever.

Wes, Adam, and Trey would say I just need a good fuck. Maybe that's all they would need, but if they were honest with themselves, they'd admit that it would break them if their relationships ended.

All of them have been in their relationships for too long. Well, maybe not Trey. He likes playing the field now. Thankfully, now that Forest has Ella and has found Jax, he's no longer on the "lets get Calla laid" train.

Five miles later, the burn radiating around my thighs is the least of my concerns. My legs feel like Jell-O, and the thumping of my heart feels like it might pry open my chest cavity. I slowly come to a stop and stretch at the front of my Jeep, trying to loosen the muscles a little more before they get stiff. I notice there are a few more people out on the trail today than there are normally. Not as many as the weekend brings out, but for a Wednesday, it's definitely more than usual. One jogger makes eye contact with me as he heads toward his vehicle parked two spaces away. I throw him a smile, as I pull open the car door and hop in.

———

TWO HOURS after leaving my apartment, I arrive back home. The elevator seems to drag as I ride up to my floor. After my ten-mile run with my thighs burning and calves aching, I'm dead on my feet. In an attempt to stay upright, I lean against the back corner. *At the rate this elevator is moving, I could fall asleep standing here and still not miss my floor.*

Even being this tired, I don't trust falling asleep. Not after seeing that woman rise off Torrance in my dream and walk naked out of our bedroom, as he is yelling for her to get the chocolate syrup. The nightmare always ends after my shock and outrage, but before I tell him to get the hell out. Granted, after that, I'd stormed into our room, grabbed a bag and some clothes, and headed to Adam and Nessa's house.

An audible ding fills the space, pulling me out of my head as the elevator finally stops on my floor. I stagger out and turn toward my loft. No one brushes past me on their way into the elevator like they normally do after I come home from a run, but today I did leave a good bit earlier than usual. Halfway down the hallway, I stop and bend over to pick up the paper that's laying on the mat in front of my door. As I try to straighten, my legs begin to shake, making me use the door for balance before I'm able to stand upright. Pulling my keys out, I open the door.

The sun shines brightly through my floor-to-ceiling windows, lighting the industrial loft I love so much. Sometimes I'm grateful Torrance cheated on me. *Sometimes.* If he hadn't cheated, I wouldn't have this gorgeous place overlooking downtown Austin. It's just what I'd been searching for before Torrance asked me to move in with him. Now, I have just about everything I've ever wanted.

As I shuffle in the door, I'm assaulted with soft head butts to my calves, along with an endless supply of chatter from my cat, Bagheera.

"Morning, handsome," I greet him, as I lean down and run my fingers over his silky, black fur.

"Meow." He nudges my hand, soaking up all the attention he possibly can.

"Are you hungry?"

"Meow." His tail swishes back and forth, curling into a question mark at the tip.

I straighten and slowly step away from the door, being sure I close it completely so Baggie can't escape. I head toward the kitchen, trying not to trip over him as he continues to butt his head against my legs.

"Guess you are hungry."

"Meow."

Baggie keeps nudging me as he circles himself around my legs. I almost trip over him when we get close to the kitchen, but manage to catch myself before face-planting into the wall.

"Bagheera!" I glare down at him.

"Meow."

"Come here you little shit." As I pick him up, he starts rubbing his head against my chin. I kiss his head, and he jumps down after one last nustle.

Baggie reaches the kitchen first, jumping up on the counter next to the pantry where his food is hidden from his greedy paws. Stepping into the large gourmet kitchen area, I bend down and pick up the empty, small steel bowl that sits between the kitchen and dining room. He yowls at me as I slowly make my way down to the pantry where he waits. He yowls again as I'm scooping out his cat food. Being an impatient imp, and letting me know I'm not moving fast enough, he aims to get his head into the bag of food. When I push him out of the way, he nips at my hand, and I swat at him.

Baggie takes the hint and scampers out of the pantry. I

finish scooping all his food into his bowl, walk it back to the end of the counter, and place it next to the water bowl on the floor. As soon as he takes his first bite, he immediately starts purring. Sliding to the floor next to him, I begin stroking his sleek fur.

When my stomach begins growling, I push myself off the floor and make my way to the refrigerator. This kitchen almost tops mine at Belladonna... *almost*. It's a cook's wet dream come true, with all stainless-steel appliances, a gas stove, and granite countertops. Opening one of the side-by-side doors of the fridge, I reach in to gather the ingredients for my breakfast. An omlet sounds good after my punishing run earlier, so I grab the carton of brown eggs, turkey sausage, sharp white cheddar cheese, and the fresh salsa from my favorite Mexican restaurant.

Ingredients in hand, I step over to the counter next to the stove. After placing all the ingredients on the counter, I reach into the cabinet to my right and remove my favorite steel mixing bowl and set it next to the food. Whisk in hand, I begin creating my omelet. I whisk two eggs, season them with sea salt and coarse black pepper, chop the turkey sausage, and grate the cheese. Moving the stainless-steel skillet I always leave on the stove to the bottom right burner, I flip the gas burner on and drizzle two tablespoons of extra virgin olive oil into the skillet and let it heat.

As the oil and skillet heat, I toss the turkey sausage in. Mouthwatering smells begin to permeate my kitchen, and I add my remaining ingredients. Normally, I am able to determine when my breakfast is done by the savory smell alone. But not today, because I'm not really paying attention. Suddenly, a burnt egg smell wafts from the skillet, turning my stomach. Dry heaves quickly follow.

"Damn it!" With a flip of my wrist, I turn off the burner and throw the skillet into the sink.

I stalk out of the kitchen, balling my hands into fists and kicking off my shoes. The workout clothes I still have on are still drenched in sweat and clinging to my body. Unclenching my fists, I fumble to grab the bottom edge of my gray and pink tank top. With two tugs, I remove the sweaty, clingy shirt and throw it in the laundry room as I pass the open door. I keep moving toward my bedroom while removing one sock at a time, stumbling a few steps and trying not to fall into the walls. Safely in my bedroom, I step into my bathroom and fight with my black sports bra for an entire three minutes before it gives up it's tight grip on me. Thankfully, my gray cropped pants and black hipsters slide off me easily and onto the floor.

Walking to the shower, I turn the faucet all the way to the left and step in. I stand under the spray waiting for the water to warm from cold to hot in hopes that it will relax my stiff muscles. Ten glorious minutes under the relaxing spray pass before the cleaning ritual starts; washing my face, shampooing my hair, shaving, rinsing my hair and conditioning it, washing my body, and rinsing everything off. My actions are mechanical as I zone out and let my body take over. I'm still zoned out as I step out of the shower and grab my towels.

After quickly wrapping my hair in one towel, I hurriedly dry off with the other while steam still hangs in the room, keeping me warm. As I open the bathroom door and move back into my room toward my closet, the heat from my shower rushes out with me. All dry and hair still contained, I peer into my closet contemplating my outfit for the day.

"Jeans and layered t-shirts," I murmur to myself and grab the closest pair of jeans and two tees; one heather gray with long sleeves, and the other a short-sleeved pale steel blue.

Clothes in hand, I step from the closet, toss the shirts and jeans on the bed, and head over to my dresser that sits between the closet and bathroom. *Now, to pick out the perfect bra and underwear for my outfit.* I've felt compelled to match my undergarments to my clothing since I was young, and to this day, I can't stop. It's much like how I feel compelled to keep my closet and kitchen meticulously organized. Everything has a certain spot and a certain direction it has to face. I call it OCD, but my friends with psychology degrees disagree. *Whatever. It still isn't normal.*

Fully dressed, I head back into the bathroom to finish getting ready. The last routine of my morning is to fix my hair. I finish towel-drying it and spray it with leave-in conditioner before blowing it dry. Curling the ends and wrapping it up in a bun, I am armed and ready for the rest of my day. On my way out of my loft, I stop at the kitchen bar to scratch Baggie's head and kiss his little pink nose before walking to the front door.

As I leave my apartment building I notice that even this

late in the morning, people are still bustling about. The air holds onto a chill, which is odd this early in Austin's fall season. Fall usually doesn't start until late October here, and it's only mid-September. Even with the chill, I decide to walk to work, stopping at the neighborhood coffee shop to grab breakfast.

CHAPTER 2

CALLA

With four cups of specialty coffee, my chai tea, muffins, and a box of fresh gourmet coffee in hand, I arrive at Belladonna about twenty minutes later. As I lean against the door to stabilize everything and grab my keys from my pocket, it swings open, and I all but fall inside. Juggling the coffee as not to spill any, I heave a huge sigh. Taking a deep breath, I resign myself not to explode at the first person I come in contact with. The stress of the unlocked door before business hours is currently the least of my issues. Besides, the guys are here somewhere. And I'm pretty confident that Adam keeps a baseball bat behind the bar, as he's said so on multiple occasions. He wants the girls to have protection on the nights they close alone.

Sunlight pours in from the windows and skylights. That,

along with the mood lighting over the bar, and by the wood burning flat-bread oven, are the only lights on in the restaurant. The open concept, allowing people to see a little of what is going on in the kitchen, had not been my idea. In the beginning, I fought against having it. But between Trey, Wes, Wes's brothers Sam and Noel, my brother Ben, and Torrance, the concept took shape. I have to admit that it does soften the exposed stone walls and the slate bar and counter tops. The extra light from all the windows and skylights also helps to soften the overall look of the restaurant.

The front-of-the-house staff continue to bustle about and don't acknowledge me when I come in, even with all the racket I'm making. I place my breakfast, along with the treats and coffee I've gotten for the kitchen staff, on the hostess stand and turn back to lock the door.

It isn't until I get close to the bar that someone finally perks up and comes to help me. Adam, my bar manager, and one of only a few people I trust completely, is at my side in a few quick strides. He takes his cup out of the holder, as he picks up the box of fresh coffee from the stand.

"Calla, what are you doing here? Didn't we tell you to take the day off?" he questions in a growly voice, frowning down at me.

Over the years, he's become like a brother to me, and his wife, Nessa, a sister. On that disastrous night a year ago, it was their house I ran to. I knew they'd take me in and be of comfort without any tension like Wes or Trey's places would've created.

Wes, Trey, and Forest are the other men I trust completely. They are presumably in the kitchen at this time of the day. Well, Forest isn't. He's still on vacation with his daughter, Ella.

Adam stands almost eye-level with me at his five-foot-eight height as I look him over. Today he is wearing gray slacks and a rich blue button-up shirt, with the top two buttons unbuttoned. With his sleeves rolled up to his elbows, he's showing off the ink on his right forearm. It all looks good on his lean frame, and the blue shirt draws out his stormy blue eyes.

Damn! Nessa has great taste in clothes. One of these days, I may finally let her take me shopping. Though, when would I wear anything she'd pick out? I'm always in jeans and my coat.

"Yes, the three of you did tell me to take the day off, but I have too many things to do here." I keep walking while taking the first sip of my chai.

"Wes and Trey aren't going to be happy. It's like you don't trust us."

I snort. "Should I?" I tease. "Yes, I've known you guys for years. And you know I trust all of you. But what is it, exactly, that you want me to do tonight?"

He knows I trust them completely. He also knows I am still on the fence about dating again. All of them, including Nessa, have been pushing me to date since six weeks after "the incident." I haven't been able to, though. Since that night, I haven't fully trusted myself in any aspect of my life, and it is showing in everything I cook.

Adam's cheeks flush, and I conclude that the "boys" have been talking about me. Again.

"Which one of you three said something? Don't answer that! Let me guess...Wes." I roll my eyes. "It went something like this, right? 'It's been too long. She needs to get laid.'" My voice drops a few octaves to match Wes's pitch.

Laughter erupts from Adam's throat. "You nailed it!" He grins and winks. "Seriously, we want you to take the night off. Honestly, I don't care what you do, just do something fun. We'll take care of everything. I'll even call Nessa and see if she can help out in the kitchen if you want."

"Fine. But I do have a few things to get done here this morning. Also, I think I want us to have a meeting sometime in the next few days. Something needs to change." I murmur the last few words, hoping Adam doesn't hear.

"Calla, we are willing to do whatever is needed to make you happy, and to get you out of the rut you're in."

"Thank you." My eyes start to sting, as I fight back the tears.

I need to put in a few orders for the rest of the week and make sure the meat is fresh for the next two nights. But after hearing Adam say they have my back, and fighting off the tears, I am ready to turn tail and run. I hate disappointing my friends, and hopefully, soon-to-be business partners. Yes, Belladonna is my baby, but Adam, Forest, Trey, and Wes didn't have to stay with me, nor did they have to join me when I'd told them two-and-a-half years ago what I wanted to do. They'd wanted in back then, but now I'm not holding up my end of the bargain.

I could let Trey and Wes make the orders. They've done that before. But that feels like I'm giving up completely, and I can't do that.

Last night I'd decided I was actually going to listen to the guys and take the day off, but I want to talk to them about what to do with my time away from this place. I can't even remember the last time I actually went out, not to mention, the last time I went on a date.

My cheeks puff up before I let out a long, audible huff of air.

Adam keeps up with my tension-laden pace as we walk through the drink station and into the kitchen. Trey and Wes are working on their opening duties as we prepare for the rest of the staff to arrive for their shifts.

"Hey, Calla!" someone calls out from the far side of the kitchen.

"Morning," I respond out of habit.

Two tall, well-toned bodies stop in the middle of the kitchen and move in the opposite direction from the rest of the staff.

"Hey, cutie. What are you doing here?" Trey's deep, smooth voice filters over all the kitchen commotion.

"Checking in." The words come out quick and without thought.

"You could've just called." There is censure in his tone.

"Yeah, yeah, I know. Can we talk in the office, please?" At

my words, Wes side-steps toward me. "I did bring coffee and muffins." I put the muffins down on a prep table on my way to our office.

Adam follows my lead and sets the container of coffee down next to the bag I'd carried. With his hand now free, he reaches in the bag and pulls out one of the strawberry muffins I picked up for him.

"Will one of you grab me a muffin?" Wes asks, as he walks toward the office.

"No problem. Calla, how many did you bring?" Adam inquires.

"There should be two for each of you."

A ripping sound comes from behind me. Glancing back, I see the bag is torn open, and the muffins lay strewn on the table.

Trey and Adam follow me toward the far back corner of the kitchen next to the freezer. Wes already has the office door unlocked and propped open. He sits at his desk, waiting. As I enter, he stands.

It still amazes me that we are able to fit our four desks comfortably in this space. It's a minimalist space without frills. The desks all have sleek glass tops and adjustable legs, so we can either stand or sit. We each have a set of small file cabinets underneath, and laptops are sitting out on the desk tops. Well, all but mine, as my laptop is in the bag I have slung over my shoulder.

"Hey, Wes? Coffee." I hold out the cup holder that still has two large brown paper cups toward him.

"Thanks, Calla." Wes takes the one closest to him.

As Trey moves to his desk, he grabs the last cup from the holder. I toss the cup-carrier in the trash before taking my seat. The room remains silent as I put my breakfast on my desk and remove my laptop from my bag. With everything set out on my desk, I take a sip of my chai and swivel to face my friends.

"What's up babe?" Wes asks around his cup.

"I'm just going to make the orders for the weekend and Tuesday, then I'll get out of your hair."

"Why didn't you just do that from home?" Trey questions.

"I wasn't sure what all we needed. I was so tired last night, I forgot to check before I left. And I know I could've called, but you guys have been covering my ass for months. Doing the orders is the one thing I haven't screwed up since Torrance." Embarrassment, anger, and pain combine, causing me to look away from my friends.

They've never judged me for what happened. Or for how I've coped, or not coped, with "the incident" no one speaks of. Though, all four of these guys, along with some of the other staff, did threaten to kick Torrance's ass if he ever stepped foot in Belladonna again.

"Calla, you were engaged to that son-of-a-bitch. The fact that you didn't kill him that night is a miracle, so we can deal with how you've coped. Do we want our fun-loving, kick-ass, lead chef back? I'm not going to lie. We definitely do." Trey smirks and takes a sip of his coffee.

"Alright sweetie, what's going on? Why are you feeling so blue today?" Adam asks.

"This morning I tried to make breakfast again. And failed. Again. And I keep having the damn nightmare every night. Me walking in on Torrance and his mistress...."

"Fuck! That son-of-a-bitch is still causing problems. You should've let me kick his ass," Wes fumes.

"That wouldn't have accomplished anything. I needed you in the kitchen and not charged with assault." I tear apart my muffin and stuff a piece in my mouth.

"She has a point, Wes. We needed you here. I would have asked one of my brothers to do it, though. They fight for a living," Trey reminds us, as he re-adjusts his stance to lean against his desk.

"I know, and I appreciate that. But that's not why I wanted to talk to you guys this morning. I'd like your help in revamping this place. Torrance had too much influence when we created it, so I want to make it strictly ours now, without any trace of him in here, whatsoever. Can you start writing down ideas for what you want to see changed? New menu ideas, uniforms... whatever you can think of. And when Forest gets back, let's be sure to tell him about this. I'm sure he'll want to change up the desserts. Maybe we can get Ella to make some suggestions, too. "

They make eye contact with each other, then with me.

"Deal!" they announce at the same time.